ALLEGHENY HIDEAWAY

KIMBERLY GORDON

Energion Publications
Gonzalez, FL 32560
2012

Cover Design: Henry Neufeld
Cover Art: Josh Green

ISBN10: 1-938434-11-0
ISBN13: 978-1-938434-11-2
Library of Congress Control Number: 2012949976

Dedication

This book is dedicated to every woman who has suffered any form of abuse. My heart goes out to you. If you are not in a safe place, get to a safe place. God wants good things for us, and that includes a happy future. A portion of the profits from this book will be donated to a safe house for women and children.

TABLE OF CONTENTS

1

March 15, 1861

Missus Iris Elaine Picket sat in front of her beautifully carved walnut vanity. Her sad blue eyes cast a slow glance downward. Long black hair hung to her waist. Bringing young hands of only twenty-one years to her face, Iris cried salty tears. She was so sad. Just days before, her life had seemed so gay for the first time in a year and a half. Johnathan Wayne Picket had been a good husband, for a few weeks, but after that first month of marriage, his hot temper had emerged. It was now his habit to hit and slap her, often. And he said cruel things.

Iris rubbed the ache in her abdomen. Only a week before, she had carried a very small new life in her body. She had been so excited about having a baby. But before she could tell Johnathan, he had punched her in the stomach twice. Needless to say, later that night, she had lost the baby. Ever since then, her days were filled with dread and tears wondering how she could ever escape.

Iris looked up as her bedroom door squeaked. Her colored twenty year old maid, Hattie, walked into the room. Hattie had been a wedding gift from Iris' mother in Charleston.

"You feelin' sick again, Missus Iris?" the young woman asked.

"Shut the door Hattie," Iris spoke gently. Once the door was closed, Iris spoke again. "No Hattie, I'm not sick. Just sad." She could talk to Hattie. They were friends. Iris didn't have many friends. Johnathan didn't allow her out much for social visits. He insisted that her place was in the home.

"How'd you want me to fix your hair tonight?" Hattie asked softly.

"I don't care. Just put it up." Tonight was one of those rare occasions when she and Johnathan were going to a party together. It was a celebration at a nearby cotton plantation. Johnathan was the local crop broker for Lexington, South Carolina. He made quite good money, despite his temper. She and Johnathan lived in a rather comfortable two story home in town.

Iris looked at herself in the mirror while Hattie worked on her hair. She noticed puffiness around both eyes.

"I'm going to need some cool water for my face Hattie, or everyone will know I've been crying," she confessed.

"Yes'm."

"What am I going to do, Hattie? If I stay here, he'll kill me."

Hattie pursed her lips. "Missus Iris, if I was you, I'd kill him first … or run away. Or both," she added with a tiny snicker.

Iris grinned out of the corner of her mouth. She had had murderous thoughts too, but reality cautioned otherwise. "If I killed him Hattie, the law would hang me."

"You could run away then, like them slaves do that get beat all the time," she told her mistress.

Iris looked at Hattie through the reflection in the mirror and asked, "How do you know about that?"

Hattie raised an eyebrow and smiled. "I hears things."

"You do, huh? Well, you had better keep that one to yourself. Don't ever let Mister Picket hear you say that."

"Yes, ma'am."

Iris thought for a moment while Hattie finished putting up her hair. "You know, that's not a bad idea, Hattie. I could run away. You would have to come too though," Iris informed her.

"I got no ties here," Hattie answered. "Where would we go?"

Iris shook her head. "I don't know. He'd find me. It would have to be far away."

"We could go back to Charleston and live with your mama. I like her," the slave admitted freely.

Iris shook her head again. "That would be the first place he'd look." No more was spoken on the subject by either young woman that afternoon. Iris pulled on a pretty lilac-colored gown to wear to the party. Her corset was not pulled completely tight since her stomach was still sore from losing the child.

Johnathan met her downstairs. His brown hair was combed back and he wore a fine black suit. He certainly looked like a gentleman. "Ready to go, Missus Picket?" he asked eagerly.

"Yes."

"You look lovely tonight," he spoke, planting a kiss on her cheek. "Shall we?"

Iris and Johnathan arrived at the large brick mansion around seven-thirty. It was all aglow with candles. Fifty people milled about, drinking spirits and enjoying the food. Iris saw a small group of three women that she knew and excused herself to go visit.

"Be a good girl tonight," Johnathan whispered before he would let her walk away.

At nine o'clock, the frivolity increased as a band began to play. Iris and Johnathan danced several times. Iris dared not dance with anyone else, even though she was asked and rudely had to turn them down. Johnathan danced with quite a few women; apparently he was a popular choice for the ladies.

Just around ten fifteen, Iris' stomach began to ache terribly. "It must be from the dancing," she told her husband. "Will you take me home, please?"

"Why, my dear? The party has just begun!" he stated with annoyance.

"But Johnathan, I hurt," she spoke with whispered fervor.

"Go sit down for a while. If you still hurt in an hour, we'll go then," he decreed with callousness.

Knowing he would not yield, Iris went to a chair near a front corner. For fifteen minutes she went unnoticed. She fought back tears of loneliness and pain.

"May I be of some service to you, Missus Picket?" a young man asked at last. He was one of the men she had previously turned down for a dance.

"Please, sir, find my husband. I am ill and really must get home," she asked of him.

"Right away, ma'am."

Iris leaned her head against the wall as the young man disappeared into the crowd. She guessed him to be about her age. After five minutes, he returned with furrowed brows.

"I am sorry, Missus Picket. Your husband is quite grossly engaged in a game of cards. He did however give me leave to escort you home. With your permission, ma'am," he said most sincerely.

Hoping her husband would not turn on her later for accepting, Iris agreed. "Thank you, sir. I would be most obliged."

The young man summoned his family carriage. While they waited, he introduced himself.

"Missus Picket, my name is Samuel B. Reed. My father is in the lumber business."

Iris extended her hand. "It is very nice to meet you, Mister Reed."

"I am sorry you are not feeling well, ma'am. But you will be home resting before you know it." On the outside, Samuel was being polite. On the inside, he wanted to strangle Mister Picket for abandoning his wife in her time of need.

Iris smiled to herself. How nice this young man was to come to her rescue. When the coach arrived, Samuel helped her inside. The cushions were covered in velvet.

"To Lexington," Samuel told his driver.

As the coach drove her home, Iris searched her mind for something to say. "Mister Reed, you mentioned your father was in the lumber business. Was he at the party too?"

"No, ma'am. He's visiting my grandmamma in Pennsylvania. She lives in a little town up near the Allegheny Mountains called Williamsport," he replied. "Ever heard of it?"

Iris laughed quietly. "Well, actually, no. But I'm sure it's a very nice place."

"Oh, it is," he answered quickly. "It's a beautiful little town in the mountains with a big river running just south. I'll go back one day."

Iris smiled at him in the darkness. "Are you from there? How did you end up way down South?"

"My father's family is from there. My mother's was from Maryland. I've been all over, going with my father where the work goes. Right now, we are harvesting some land …" his voice trailed off. "Do you really want to hear this?"

She smiled slightly. "Do go on."

Samuel shifted in his seat. "Well, to keep it simple, we are clearing forest here. But the main reason we moved south is for my mother. She hated the cold winters."

"Is she with your father then, up north?" Iris asked.

"No, ma'am. Not this trip. You see, she died last year."

Iris regretted the question. "Oh. I'm very sorry. My father died when I was ten. But my mother remarried. She and Tom live in Charleston."

The remainder of the drive into town was uneventful as Iris and Samuel spoke about families. When they reached her doorstep, he politely assisted her out of the coach. While her hand was still in his, he bent down to offer it a kiss. "If you ever need help again ma'am, or a friend, please call on me," he offered.

Iris was genuinely touched by his sincerity and manners. What a wonderful person he was. "Thank you very much, Mister Reed," she told him with gratefulness.

Martin, the Picket's doorman, opened the front door. Iris thanked her escort and went inside.

After a good night's rest, Iris awoke with a plan. She knew now what needed to be done to protect herself from Johnathan's anger. She had to run away; she had to leave and go far. And now, after the conversation with Samuel Reed, she knew where to go. Johnathan would never dream that she would move north. And he would never set foot on Northern soil to come find her. Iris made up her mind to make a plan and leave this very week.

That night at the dinner table, Iris and Johnathan were having a quiet meal when Iris put her plan into action. Butterflies in her stomach churned wildly, but she forced herself to look calm on the outside.

"Johnathan dear, I would like to go and visit my mother," she began.

"What for?" he barked. "All she will do is try to convince you to stay in the city when you know you belong here." His eyebrows furrowed angrily.

"Yes, I know. But we haven't been there since last summer and I would like to go in the spring before it gets too hot. I can take Hattie and stay for just two weeks. That would make me happy. You don't care do you?" She held her breath for his answer.

"I suppose I really don't care one way or the other," he said sarcastically. "But I'm not going. You can stay for two weeks, but after that, you come right back," he ordered.

Iris nodded, not trusting her voice to speak. She could not believe her good fortune. It had been easier than she thought.

Later that night, Iris secretly began sewing hidden pockets into the folds of her petticoats. After three more days, she was packed and ready. All of her jewelry was secretly stashed away into the folds. She would sell them as money was needed.

As her trunk was lifted onto the back of the wagon, she and Johnathan climbed into the coach. Hattie, with her one bag, climbed onto the wagon. They had a ten mile ride to Columbia. Iris had warned Hattie to say absolutely nothing about their plans.

She told her to act normal, that they were just going on a visit to Charleston.

Iris' cream and peach colored dress echoed her cheerful spirits as the coach pulled up to the train station in Columbia on this pretty spring day. Once on the platform, Johnathan handed her a ten dollar bill.

"Just a little money in case you do something stupid and get into trouble," he told her. "Be careful in Charleston. Don't be seen where you shouldn't be. I have friends down there who will be watching out for you," he advised. He then turned to Hattie. "Don't you be uppity to your mistress now, just because she's taking you on a trip. Understand?" he asked.

"Yes, sir," Hattie answered obediently with a nod of her scarf-covered head.

Iris nearly jumped out of her shoes as the train whistle blew from nearby. It would depart in just minutes and she would be free at last.

"Take care while I'm gone," she told her husband, trying to act normal. "I'll be back two weeks from today."

Johnathan gave her a quick kiss goodbye. "I'll sure be lonely at night while you're gone," he whispered quietly. "But we can make up for it when you get back," he added with a wink.

Inside, Iris was repulsed at the thought. For appearances though, she smiled and tried to act embarrassed.

"All aboard," came the call from the man down the line.

Iris watched as her trunk was loaded. She turned to Hattie. "You go on down to your car now. I'll see you in Charleston." Hattie took her bag and headed toward the back of the train.

"Goodbye, Johnathan," Iris spoke demurely.

"Bye, Iris. See you soon," he answered.

Iris gripped her closed parasol tightly and entered the train with strong reserve. This was her freedom, this was her escape. She took a seat on the far side of the car so Johnathan would not be able to see her as the train pulled away. She never even looked back to see if he remained on the platform. The whistle blew again and she could hear the captain shouting. Her heart beat wildly. Finally, the train began to pull away. *"Goodbye, cruel Johnathan,"* she thought in her mind. *"You'll never see me again."*

Iris sat mostly still for the first twenty-five miles of the trip, trying to accept that her surroundings were for real. But after the stop in Kingsville, she began to smile. It was real. It was wonderfully real. The train crossed the bridge over the Congaree River and headed south to Orangeburg. Iris enjoyed the scenery as distance was gained from her past. She chatted easily with a few of the fellow passengers. One family of six was traveling to the seashore for a holiday. Many passengers were men on business. Iris could tell by the way they dressed and the seriousness of their expressions. One young couple sat in the back and the woman kept giggling. Iris supposed them to be newlyweds, off on a trip. She wondered what it would have been like to be happily married. She hoped this woman had not been deceived as she had been. Johnathan had been very charming while he was courting her. It was not until after the marriage that his true nature had shown through. Iris caught herself thinking about Johnathan and resolved not to give him further thought for a long time.

The South Carolina Railroad steamed through Branchville, St. Georges and several other small towns before finally reaching Charleston. Iris was so thrilled to breathe in salty ocean air once more. This was her real home. She searched the crowd on the platform to find her mother and Tom. Tom had been good to her in the seven years they had known one another, and it was obvious that he loved her mother. She knew her mother would always be in good hands.

The train entered the large train yard where several lines of tracks came together bringing people and products from north, west, and south. Iris collected her lace trimmed parasol and exited the train. She entered the throng of people on the platform. It was hard to move around at times, with all the women in wide hooped skirts, but at last she heard a familiar voice cry out.

"Iris!" her mother shouted.

Iris turned to that wonderful sound and saw her mother waving arms above her head. She smiled at the wonderful sight. It was like pure medicine to see her loving face again. Iris waved back and headed in her direction.

"It's so good to see you!" her mother said with relief as they embraced.

"It's good to be home, Mother. I'm so glad to be here," she answered, nearly crying with happy emotions.

"What about me?" Tom teased. Both women snickered.

"Hello, Tom. It's good to see you too," Iris answered, giving him a hug as well.

"You look more like your mama every year it seems," Tom said with a smile. "Pretty as ever!"

Both women exchanged a glance and grinned. Tom had been saying that for six years. "Let's go home," he then suggested.

"Wait. Hattie is here," Iris explained. "We need to find her."

Tom stood on his toes to look over the crowd. "I think I see her just getting off now."

"Can you wave at her?" Iris asked.

Tom caught Hattie's attention. The slave walked over to the family with her bag in hand.

"Hello again, Hattie," Iris' mother, Savannah, told the maid.

"Hello, Missus Payton. Mister Payton," she answered with a curtsey.

Tom nodded a response, then turned to his stepdaughter. "Which one is your trunk, Iris?"

"The one with purple straps."

After searching for the trunk, the group climbed into a waiting carriage to make the drive home. Hattie sat up front with the driver and was perfectly content with the scenery.

"It's so good to have you back," Savannah told her daughter. "I wish you could stay for more than two weeks though. That's just hardly any time at all!"

Iris grimaced. She had not yet told her mother anything about Johnathan's abuse and her real intentions for this visit. She would break it to her parents tonight after dinner and leave the day after tomorrow. It would be hard to say goodbye, but necessary.

Tom's carriage pulled into the drive. He was a local merchant and made a comfortable living for himself and Savannah. Their brick home featured both an upper and lower porch facing east and a cool shade covered garden down the north side of the home. Iris could have lived here forever. It was such a pleasant way of life.

Dinner was served on the upper porch. It consisted of crab cakes, baked flounder stuffed with onions and breading, rice and spices and green beans topped with almonds. Dessert was a special tropical pudding with coconut and pineapple.

"Bought the fruit right off the ship from the islands," Tom told her proudly.

"It's absolutely delicious!" Iris complimented after the first bite. What a wonderful feast this had been. The perfect meal to remember for a long time.

Shortly after dinner was over and the dishes had been cleared by servants, Iris' thoughts returned to her plan. With a deep, brave breath, she began.

"I sure wish I could stay and enjoy everything that you and Charleston have to offer. I could be so happy here …" She looked dreamily off the balcony at the pretty yard below.

Savannah frowned. "What do you mean, honey? Aren't you happy in Lexington with Johnathan?"

Iris took another deep breath. "Well, actually Mama, no. I'm not."

With both their attentions, Iris explained to her mother and Tom all that had transpired recently, including the loss of her baby. She then outlined her plan to leave the day after tomorrow and escape once and for all.

"Oh, no! Iris, you can't just leave like that," Savannah spoke with alarm.

"I'll just go kill him!" Tom stated angrily.

"I've thought of that too Tom, but the law would hang us," Iris cautioned him sensibly.

"It's not right," Savannah uttered as she began to cry. "He's the one ought to be hanged."

"I know Mama, I know," Iris answered with a hug. "But they won't. And if I asked him for a divorce, he wouldn't let me have one, and I would be disgracing the family. If I moved here, he would simply come and get me. Then I'd really be beaten. So my only choice really is to just disappear."

Tom was deep in thought as his wife spoke her fears.

"Surely there must be another way," Savannah sighed. She was terrified at the thought of losing her only child.

"Mama, he even has spies here in Charleston. He said they would be watching me."

"What if I threatened him?" Tom offered.

"Thank you Tom, but I don't think it would matter to him. His heart is cruel. He's an evil nature none of us saw before it was too late. I just have to leave him," Iris spoke solemnly. "Or fake my own death, but that could get complicated …"

Grasping for hope, Savannah asked, "Why do you have to leave the day after tomorrow? Johnathan knows you're going to be here for two weeks. Why can't you just leave then?"

Iris smiled at her mother sympathetically. "Because I need a head start Mama, to make it harder for him to track me."

"What will you use to get by? Where will you go? What will you do?" Tom wondered, trying to help her with a solution.

"I have all my jewelry sewn into my clothes. I plan to sell it when I need money," she confessed.

Tom nodded. "But it won't last forever, Iris. What will you do then?"

Iris raised her hands in gesture. "I will work."

Savannah made a noise in her throat at the thought of her lovely daughter working. "Where?" she asked.

"I don't yet know that, Mama. It just depends," she answered honestly. "I don't have my whole plan thought out yet, but I'm working on it."

Tom didn't like any of it, not one bit. He might even have to put his foot down. "Where will you go?"

Iris looked him in the eye. "I have an idea, but I want to keep it a secret. I don't even want you both to know where I am, in case Johnathan tries to get it out of you."

Savannah scoffed. "He'd have to kill me first!"

"He might try, Mother. That's why I won't tell you."

"Then how will I know if you are safe? I won't be able to sleep at night," Savannah complained. What could she say to keep her daughter close?

"I have a letter on me that says who I really am and who you are. If anything bad happens to me, you will be notified. If you don't hear from anyone, then you know I am safe," Iris answered factually. She had put a lot of thought into these things as well.

Savannah brought her hand up to her head and cried. "Oh Iris!"

Tom came over for support. He looked at Iris. "I understand why you want to do this, Iris. But I want to give this some thought overnight and see if I can't come up with another plan for you. Are you sure you don't want me to go to the authorities, or talk to Johnathan myself?"

"Please Tom, don't bother. I want to leave," she admitted humbly. "I want to go far away and start over somewhere where nobody knows me. You two are the only people I have to leave behind, but I'll be back. Someday … I hope."

Savannah quietly wept real tears as she thought of her daughter's terrible situation. What could she do to help?

All business, Iris turned to Tom. "Tomorrow, will you please ask one of your employees to purchase a ticket for me on a ship to Wilmington? Give him another name to use, I can't go as myself. One of Johnathan's spies might recognize me. I need a ticket for Hattie as well."

Suddenly, Savannah shouted out, "A wig and a veil!"

Tom and Iris both turned to her.

Savannah lowered her voice. "Iris, I have a blond wig that I wore to a masquerade ball several years ago. You could wear it. I also have a black hat and a veil you could use to cover your face."

"That would be wonderful, Mother," Iris agreed. "Do you have a black dress I could wear? I could go as a widow. That would really throw them off."

"Actually dear, I do. It's very dated though, from when your father died."

"Even better," Iris smiled. "With gloves on, they will think I'm an old lady."

Tom snorted. "Very funny," Savannah spoke sarcastically.

Realizing what she had said, Iris began to giggle. "Sorry, Mother. I didn't mean it that way."

Tom still grinned. "It is a good idea though. It's a great disguise."

Later that evening, after the sun was down, Savannah took Iris up to her room. "Honey, you know I hate to see you go," she spoke quietly. "But I know that you must. I want to help you any way I can. I want you to have some things."

Savannah went over to her jewelry box and pulled out several precious items: two rings, a pearl necklace, garnet earbobs, two cameos, and a gold brooch. She also pulled out several silver coins.

"Oh Mother, I couldn't," Iris protested.

"But Daughter, if it will help save your life … I would hate myself if I didn't give these things to you. They are small and will travel easily in your clothes. They will bring you more money if you need it." She handed the items to her daughter. "The only advice I can give you is to try and invest some of the money you have left when you get where you're going. Find a way to make money with your money. And be very careful with whom you invest. A woman can't trust just anybody," she explained wisely.

Iris gave her mother a loving embrace. "Thank you, Mama. You're so wonderful." After a moment, Iris added, "You know I hate to leave you."

"You will come back one day though, won't you?" Savannah asked. "Or at least let me know where you are and if you're well?"

"If I can, you know I will."

2

The following day, Tom sent one of his employees to purchase a ticket for a Missus Samantha Jo Blackheart. The plan was for Iris to pretend to be a grieving widow. Tom went himself to purchase one for Hattie, under the name Mary Grace. She was to be his slave, being traded to a new buyer in North Carolina. It was easy enough to forge the documents. Hattie and Iris would be on the same ship, but would not see each other at all until they met at the wharves in Wilmington. Iris had the false bill of purchase for "Mary Grace." From there, Iris kept her plans to herself.

Savannah visited the store in town where she had purchased the blond wig to see if they had any more ready made. Much to her delight, there were several. She purchased one with light brown hair, and another with a reddish tint. She wanted to make sure her daughter would not be recognized anywhere. Back at home, Iris tried on all the disguises.

"I don't even recognize my own daughter!" Savannah stated, pleased with the outcome. "Remember to wear veils though, or people will see your dark eyebrows and know your hair is really black," she warned.

"I have three veils mother, plus the black one you gave me. That should be enough."

"Oh daughter, I wish you the best of luck. It is rather exciting, running off, isn't it?"

"What will you tell Johnathan, when he comes?" Iris worried.

Savannah took a breath, thinking. "If Tom doesn't shoot him first, we will just tell him nothing."

"You could always tell him you put me on the train to come home," Iris suggested. "That way, he will concentrate on those areas for a while. I will be long gone by then. He'll think someone kidnapped me. By the time he catches on and begins to look elsewhere, people will have forgotten me. Besides, his descriptions won't match up with anyone they've seen," she said smiling.

"Serves him right! I can't believe he's done this to you, honey. I wish we could go to the law. But you're right, they would side with the husband. Laws aren't made to protect women. Maybe one day … I can't believe I let you marry him," Savannah sighed, partly blaming herself for the situation.

"Mother, nobody knew. It's not your fault. Not at all."

Savannah's shoulders slumped. "I know, honey. I'm just angry."

That evening, Iris, her mother and her step-father enjoyed one last evening together before she disappeared. It was spent in both laughter and tears as they tried to savor every last moment.

After an unrestful night, everyone rose early to put the plan into action. At eight o'clock, Tom took Hattie to the shipyard to make arrangements for her travel. Hattie was a little frightened about the whole situation. She had never been on a ship before, having been born in Georgia and sent away from her mother when she was twelve to go work in Savannah. Then at seventeen, she had gone to Charleston. Tom assured her that she would be fine. Hattie was loaded into the cargo hold by nine.

At nine o'clock, Savannah sent for a hired driver. He was to deliver his widowed rider and her trunk to the stagecoach office. Meantime, Iris put on her black costume and said her tearful good-byes to her mother. When the driver came, Iris gingerly climbed into the seat. Her mother waved as the driver pulled away. Once at the stagecoach office, Iris thanked the driver and had him unload her trunk. She then went inside to pretend to purchase a ticket. After ten minutes, she summoned another driver to take her to the docks. Along the way, she talked about how she had just arrived from Savannah and that she would never take the stage again because her old bones were bounced and bruised. Once he had her delivered to the wharf, he made sure she got onto the ship in good condition.

"Thank you, young man," she told the thirty year old. Secretly, she was grinning.

Once aboard, Iris walked over to the far side of the ship to look out over the water. She had never been on a large sailing ship before either. It was scary and exciting all at the same time. She looked down at her black dress. Her masquerade was working well so far. No one had questioned her at all. She found a seat on a nearby box and decided to remain there until the vessel was out to sea. She wanted to see the ocean and enjoy all the beauty the day had in store.

At noon, a whistle blew. The crew shouted and ran about like rabbits. Ropes were pulled as the strong men lifted sails. Tarps filled with wind and billowed out with great noise. Iris felt the ship rock in the water as they pulled away from the dock. Overhead, seagulls circled the great masts calling out their cries of excitement. As the ship went through the pass, Iris watched men waving from the walls of Fort Sumter.

Today's voyage would take just one day. She wondered if she would get seasick. She had heard of that happening before, to both men and women. After waiting on the deck for a while, Iris went below to find her cabin. As she looked around the accommodating room, she thought of Hattie, who was probably stuck down below in a very small room with several other female slaves. Iris felt guilty for putting her faithful friend and servant in such a bad situation. At least it was only for one day.

The next afternoon, as the ship pulled into the slip at Wilmington, a cool spring rain began to fall. Overhead, the gray sky was heavy with clouds. Iris was thankful that the storm was just beginning. It would have made for rough seas. The trip had been pleasant enough, but she was thankful to be on dry land once again. She reached for her umbrella to keep dry. Within a minute, the steward came by to carry her trunk. She informed him that it needed to be delivered to the hotel. Once he was gone, Iris went up on deck. From what she could see, Wilmington seemed to be a quaint little town.

"Enjoy your visit, Missus Blackheart," the captain said as she stepped onto the gangplank. "Do you need any assistance getting down?"

"No, thank you, Captain," Iris answered, nodding politely. She hurried down as fast as she dared to avoid any more conversation.

Iris watched as her trunk was loaded onto a wagon and driven to the Westport Hotel just three blocks away. She quickly made the short walk and registered inside as Missus Eugene Gray. In her room, she hastily changed into a pretty colorful dress in varying shades of red. She then pulled on the light brown wig and a cute straw hat with a simple ruffle of flowers on top. Without wasting a moment, she found her receipt for Hattie and rushed back to the ship. Since no one had seen her face on board, they did not recognize her at all when she walked up to the captain.

"Excuse me sir," she called out waving.

He saw the pretty young woman below and waved back.

"Where can I pick up my new slave?" she asked, trying to act helpless as she waved her receipt.

The captain smiled and pointed a hand toward the back of the ship.

"Thank you!" Iris called out with another flirty wave.

Satisfied, she walked to the unloading area where several slaves were waiting in a pen like livestock. Some, to her horror, were even chained. Iris spotted Hattie, who did not look well. Iris quickened her steps and took her paperwork to the man who looked like he was in charge.

"Sir, I've come for my new slave," she spoke loudly.

The man gave Iris a glancing over. His eyebrow shot up with approval. "A new slave, eh?" he asked back.

"Yes. A female. I'm guessing it's that one," she said, pointing to Hattie.

The man pointed at Hattie and ordered, "Come here!" He then looked at the papers he was given back in Charleston and compared them to what he was just given. "Yeah, she's the one." The man stamped the receipt and handed the sheet back to Iris. "There you go, ma'am. Have a good day now. And if you ever need another slave, you just come see me," he added with a wink.

Iris nodded politely, but was disgusted. Hattie walked forward and Iris took her by the upper arm.

"Come with me," she ordered sternly, just for show.

When they were out of earshot, Hattie let out a breath of relief. "Ma'am, I am so glad to see you." She was almost in tears. "I's never been so scared in a long time as I was on that ship."

"You're safe again now. Remember to call me Missus Gray while we are here. On the next ship, I'll make sure you can stay with me."

Hattie made an awful face. "Do we have to go on another one?"

"I'm afraid so, but not right away," Iris answered. "Why don't we go get something to eat right now? Later we can look into the train schedule for tomorrow."

Hattie smiled. "I am awful hungry. We only got one meal, and it was terrible." The slave walked on a few more feet in silence, then asked, "Where are we goin' go on this train?"

Iris looked around. No one was listening. "Norfolk, Virginia."

On a pretty morning the following day, Iris and Hattie boarded the Wilmington and Weldon Railroad. Iris wore her red dress and light brown wig again and told Hattie to sit in the back of the train car on a special bench just for servants. They were in for a long day of traveling, with many stops along the way. Iris spent the time reading a newspaper she had purchased that morning. Hattie either visited with another maid, looked out the window, or watched the people inside the car. About supper time, the train

finally pulled into the depot at Norfolk. It was a busy little seaside
town. After de-boarding, Iris found a nice little inn. Hattie had
her own servant's room on the ground floor and was thankful for
the quiet, private space. Iris' room was on the third floor, and had
a great view of the bay. The pretty building overlooked the harbor
and served a delicious supper downstairs. Iris and Hattie went for
a short stroll after eating, to stretch their legs a bit after such a long
day in a chair.

All the little shops along the street were closed for the evening,
but the two friends enjoyed the fresh air and change of scenery.
They returned to the inn long before dark to avoid any trouble and
slept soundly.

After a hearty breakfast of corned beef over biscuits, Iris, still in
her brown wig, headed out in a peach colored dress to find a ship.
Hattie went along for protection. Unfortunately, Iris learned that
no ships were heading to Baltimore until the next day.

"Well, Hattie, uh, Mary Grace …" Iris corrected herself. They
had promised not to use their real names on this entire trip. "Looks
like we have some free time today. I think I would like to browse
around the stores. You can have a little money too if you want to
buy yourself a trinket or something."

"Thank you, ma'am," the twenty year old replied, thrilled at
the treat. "Are you sure you have enough to get us where we're
goin'?"

"Yes. Don't you worry about that. We'll be fine."

In the mercantile, Hattie picked out a bar of softly scented
soap and a small sampler to stitch. "It will give me something to do
on the ship. Plus, I would like to hang it in my new room, when
we get settled."

"That's a fine idea," Iris approved. She picked out a new pair
of soft white kid leather gloves, then paid for all the purchases.

The sales clerk noticed her accent and commented, "You're not
from around here, are you miss?"

"Why no, sir, I'm not," she answered with a smile.

"Where are you from?" he questioned nosily.

"Georgia," she fibbed. "Ever been there?"

"No miss, but if all the ladies are as lovely as you, I guess I need to go there," he teased with a grin and a wink. "What brings you all the way up here?"

Smiling sweetly, when she really wanted to bite him, Iris lied. "My parents take a holiday every spring. We visit new towns all over the country. Last year, we went all the way to Texas!"

Hattie's eyes grew wide in disbelief. Iris was getting herself in thick with this whopper.

"My word!" the young man exclaimed. "Texas huh?"

"We leave on the noon train today," Iris continued. "I think they want to go all the way to the mountains in Virginia this time."

"What a shame you aren't staying longer," the clerk told her with real disappointment on his face. "I sure would like to have seen you again in my store."

Iris shook her head, acting of course. "What a shame … I had better go now though. Papa sure won't want me missing the train. Bye," she told him with a hint of flirting.

When they were outside, Hattie scolded her mistress. "That was shameful, ma'am. You shouldn't do that. I couldn't believe those lies you told and carrying on like that …"

Iris scoffed. "He believed it. Ate up every word. Did you see it?" she almost giggled. "Really Grace, do you think he believes I'm a runaway wife with jet black hair? No. He ate up my tale and that's just what he'll repeat if he's ever asked. This is fun actually. I'm going to be a different person at each big town we stay in. It will be a detective's nightmare." Iris walked a few more steps pridefully, then added, "I'm so enjoying this freedom. I've never felt anything like it before."

"Yes, ma'am," Hattie answered. She had often wondered how it would feel to be free. It would be nice to have her freedom too.

The next morning, at seven-thirty, the ship north pulled away from port. A strong wind blew from the west. Iris had a bad feeling there would be a thunderstorm today. Wearing her reddish wig, a dark blue veil and a dark blue calico dress, she went to find the captain.

"Sir, might I inquire as to the weather today?" she asked sweetly. "Do you think we are in for a storm?"

"Ma'am," the captain answered, smiling at the pretty young woman. "You do not need to be alarmed. Our ship will slip through the waters of the Chesapeake without trouble."

"But, there is a storm brewing, is there not?" she questioned again.

"You are very bright, ma'am. Yes, there is a storm coming. Enjoy your stroll along the deck for another hour, then I would go below," he suggested.

"Thank you sir." Iris dreaded the day and went below to warn Hattie. Hattie determined to remain in their stateroom until the ship arrived in Baltimore.

"But it's nicer up on deck, Hattie, really," Iris urged. Surely Hattie preferred fresh air to stale cabin air. "That last trip was so awful for you because you were locked below. This time, you can come up with me. It's a privilege Hattie, don't pass it up. The captain said we have an hour before the storm comes."

With persuasion, Hattie joined her mistress on the upper deck. They watched as winds whipped up white caps on the water in the enormous bay. Iris visited with fellow passengers, telling them all how excited she was to be meeting up with her husband, George Whitfield, in Baltimore. Hattie grimaced every time the ship rocked.

"Mistress, I must go below," Hattie spoke fearfully after about forty minutes on deck.

"Very well. I'll be down shortly."

The storm lasted two hours. The ship rocked back and forth in the water. Lightening cracked and thunder boomed overhead. Hattie was sick more than once. Iris sat on a nearby chair and sang quietly to calm her fears. It would all be worth it, she told herself over and over.

By the time the storm ended, Hattie was in tears. "Please ma'am, no more ships," she begged. "I don't like ships."

Iris patted her on the shoulder. "No more ships, I promise. We're almost there Hattie, to where we are going. Only one more day."

"Really?" Hattie asked, relieved. "Can you tell me where it is?"

"Not yet, but I will tell you it's near some mountains. Have you ever seen a mountain?"

Hattie shook her head. "No, ma'am. You know I ain't."

"Haven't," she corrected. "Neither have I. But we will, soon."

When the sun finally came out from behind the storm clouds later that afternoon, an enormous rainbow stretched across the eastern sky. "Have you ever seen anything like it?" Iris asked her maid.

"No, ma'am. Never that big."

"It's a sign," Iris said with a smile. "Good things are ahead. Good things! It's a promise from God."

The ship pulled into the bustling city of Baltimore right about the time the sun touched the top of the treeline to the west. It cast both warm yellow light and long shadows across the streets and buildings. All the passengers eagerly walked onto dry land. Iris found a comfortable hotel and had her trunk sent ahead. While she and Hattie walked into town, Iris whispered, "It's as busy as Charleston. I think I could quite like it here."

"Is we stoppin' now?" Hattie asked hopefully.

Iris shook her head. "Not much further. Only a day, I think. I need to find a library so I can look up something on the map. I hope they're still open."

Both women worked their way through the busy streets on their way to the library. A kind man had pointed them in the right direction. Iris needed to find out exactly where Williamsport was on the map. She had written down the name of the town before leaving Lexington. That seemed so long ago ...

In the library, an older gentleman came to her aid. "How may I help you, ma'am?" he asked.

"Miss," she corrected falsely. "Miss Mamie Mayfield."

"Miss Mayfield, I am Donald Jackson. Are you looking for a particular book?"

"I am in need of a map of Pennsylvania, sir. I'm off to visit a friend in Philadelphia and I want to learn more about her state. Can you help me with that?" she asked in a sweet southern voice.

The gentleman smiled. "I'd be delighted, miss," he replied. He led her to an enormous cabinet with twenty narrow drawers. "You're not from around here."

"No sir. Alabama is my home."

"How did you end up with a friend way up in Philadelphia?" he asked curiously, making conversation.

Iris took a deep breath to stall for time while she thought up a good reason. "Well, you see sir, this great aunt of mine in Atlanta is forever trying to find me pen pals all over the country. About five years ago, she found me one in Philadelphia named Sydney Callaway and she and I have been writing like best friends ever since. She's getting married in April and I'm going up for her wedding," she finished, pleased with her answer.

"My!" the man answered, finally finding the right map in a drawer.

Iris took the map to a table and borrowed pencil and paper from another patron. She copied the map crudely, jotting down towns and streams between Baltimore and Williamsport. She had been correct, their destination was not far away. Pleased, she thanked the gentleman for his help, and left with Hattie at her heels.

"I don't know how you do that," Hattie remarked on the sidewalk. "How'd you come up with those tales?"

Iris shrugged, answering, "They just pop into my mind."

Back at the hotel, Iris signed the registry as Miss Mamie Mayfield. She and Hattie went up to the room to study their map. Iris finally showed Hattie where they were going.

"See, we get up to Harrisburg, then go north along the Susquehanna River to Williamsport. And that's where we stay," she assured her friend. "Before we left home, I met a nice young man who told me about it. His grandmother lives there. We will find her and be her friends. All I know, is that her last name is Reed."

Hattie nodded her head. "Where will we live?"

"I will find us a house and buy it," Iris promised. "I've enough money and mama told me to invest it. If I get a house with extra rooms, we can rent them out. That will give us an income so I won't have to touch our extra money."

Hattie's stomach growled loudly. Iris smiled.

"I'm hungry too, Hattie. Let's go find some food. And, you know something? I think we will stay here an extra day and rest. I want to sell some jewelry too. In a town this size, Johnathan would never be able to track me down, if he even does get this far, which I doubt."

On a beautiful spring morning two days later, Iris and Hattie found themselves on a fast moving train heading north to York, Pennsylvania. Both women found it exciting to be so far from home, yet so close to home. Iris wore her mother's blond wig and felt like a new woman entirely. Hattie felt a little new too. She knew that colored people were free in the north. She was hopeful about her own possibilities.

In York, the two women enjoyed a brief stop before traveling east to Wrightsville. From there, a coach carried them across the bridge over the Susquehanna River, then north into Harrisburg. After a good meal in a thriving teahouse, they caught another train north.

By the end of the day, Williamsport became ever closer and the mountains grew more beautiful. Both mistress and slave were thrilled at the view. At long last, the final train turned west along the riverbank tracks and headed into town.

3

Williamsport, Pennsylvania

The train whistle blew as the large machine pulled into Williamsport. Iris and Hattie were both eager to look through the glass windows at their new surroundings. The small town came into view, with scattered buildings and about a dozen or so people waiting at the station. In a word, it was quaint. The train slowed, then finally stopped before a small wooden building.

"I am free," Iris whispered under her breath. In her seat at the back of the car, Hattie thought the same thing.

Both young women left the train, carrying what bags they could. Iris instructed Hattie to wait by the trunk. "I will find someone to help, and find a place to stay," she explained.

Iris asked three people where she might stay for the night. They all told her the same thing, "There are no rooms." Iris was in tears when she returned to her only friend.

"What's the matter, ma'am?" Hattie wondered.

"There are no rooms! We've no place to stay tonight," she answered before breaking out in a great sob.

Hattie's heart pounded in fright. Would they have to sleep outside? In a strange place? There could be bad men. This was not good …

"What about that lady, ma'am? The man's grandma?"

"Maybe … She doesn't know us and I can't tell her who I really am. Or that I know her grandson. I can't tell her!" Iris answered emotionally. She had held it together all week. Why was she losing it now? "What am I going to do?"

"May I be of some service to you, ma'am?" a male voice inquired.

Both women turned at the sound. A tall man dressed in a soldier's uniform sat upon his horse. He tipped his hat at them.

"Sir, we have only just arrived and there are no rooms to rent," Iris answered. "We are stranded."

"I see," he replied calmly. "That is a problem."

"I shouldn't have come here," Iris sobbed anew. "I am being punished."

"There now, ma'am, we will find you a place to stay. Do you know anyone here?" he asked.

Iris shook her head.

"If you don't mind, may I ask why you are here?" he asked curiously.

"I'm going to live here," she answered.

"Where here?" he wondered.

"I have to buy a house," she explained.

The man on the horse looked confused. "Well, miss ..." his voice trailed off.

"Missus Blackheart, sir."

He leaned down to shake her hand. "Captain Sellers, at your service, Missus Blackheart. I know a nice elderly couple who have extra rooms. They might take you in tonight," he offered.

"Captain Sellers, we would be in your debt," Iris answered him sincerely.

The man smiled and looked ahead at a group of boys playing near the road. "Johnathan," he called out.

The hair stood up on Iris' arms at the mention of that name. But the boys began walking toward them. One in particular was about eleven and couldn't take his eyes off Hattie. When he came near, he steered clear of her.

"Johnathan, run and fetch Mister Brown's buggy. I'm taking this woman and her maid home for the night."

"Home?" Iris gulped out loud. Her heart quickened with a little fear.

"Yes, ma'am. To my folks' house. I was just on my way there myself for supper. They're good people, ma'am. You'll be safe there until you can find a house." He smiled reassuringly. "Where are you from?"

Iris gulped. "Georgia," she lied again, knowing it would be futile to try and hide her thick southern accent.

"What brings you up here?" he questioned with amusement.

"My health," she reported. Actually, that part was the truth. "The doctor told me I had to get away from the scorching hot summers."

Captain Sellers raised an eyebrow in disbelief, but he said nothing. They waited in silence until the boy returned with the borrowed buggy. Mister Brown had harnessed his horse to pull the contraption.

"Thanks Johnny," the captain told him.

"Sure Tom. You're welcome." The boy smiled at the soldier, then gave Hattie another strange look.

Hattie and Iris helped load the trunk into the wagon. The man instructed Hattie to sit on the back edge while he tied his horse to the rear. He then helped Iris into the front seat. He jumped up as well and led them to his parents' house half a mile out of town.

"Again, I thank you for your help," Iris told him.

"You're welcome, ma'am. Why are you here all alone? Where is your husband?"

Iris said a silent prayer asking God to forgive her for all the lies. She was about to tell another too. "He died at sea this winter, Captain."

"Oh. My condolences," he said somberly. "But you came up here from Georgia, all on your own?"

"Yes," was her simple reply.

Iris remained quiet. Tom thought for a moment about this woman. How very strange was her story. Hard to believe. However, he wanted to give her the benefit of the doubt, for she was quite lovely and would be staying with his parents for a short time. Fortunate for him …

Tom led the wagon into a little glen. The sky was aglow with the colors of a spring sunset as he pulled into the yard. "Here it is," he told her.

Iris looked around. It was a small farm with a lovely view.

"What do you think?" he asked.

"It's lovely, Captain," she answered honestly.

"Come inside and meet my parents. I will unload your trunk in a moment. What's your maid's name?"

"Mary Grace."

"Do come inside, both of you," he offered. "Ma? Pa?" he asked as he opened the door.

Iris saw an elderly man look up from reading a book in a large chair by the fireplace. Tom's white-haired mother came out from the kitchen, wiping her hands on an apron. She stopped in her steps and smiled when she saw their guests.

"Hello, dear. Glad you made it," she told her son. "Who's this you've brought to join us?"

"Hello, Son," his father greeted, getting up slowly from his chair. He walked closer for a handshake.

"Father, Mother, may I introduce Missus … forgive me, I have forgotten," he apologized.

"Blackheart," she answered with a slight curtsey to his parents.

Both parents nodded. "And Mary Grace," Tom finished. "Ladies, my parents, Mister and Missus Sellers."

"How do you do?" Mister Sellers questioned. He reached out to shake not only Iris' hand, but also Hattie's. Hattie was not sure how to take it, but timidly extended her hand after a panicked glace at Iris.

"Mother, Missus Blackheart needs a place to stay until she can purchase a home. I told her you had an extra room she and Mary Grace might use," Tom explained.

"Why certainly," Missus Sellers responded. "We'd be delighted to have you both. And you're just in time for supper too," she told them both with kindness. "Tom, you may put their things in the spare room," she added.

"Yes, ma'am." He left to follow her instructions.

Knowing that he could not lift anything heavy, the elder Mister Sellers offered to take Hattie's smaller bag. "Come, I'll show you your room," he told the women.

The small cabin consisted of two bedrooms off the living room, then a kitchen and dining room and a loft for storage. The bed in the spare room was homemade, from tree limbs, rope and a mattress stuffed with fabric scraps. Primitive.

"It doesn't look like much, but it's comfortable," Tom said as he entered the room with Iris' trunk. "It served my brother and me well for years."

"Thank you. It will be fine," Iris nodded appreciation.

Tom's mother arrived with a pitcher of fresh cool water. "We'll leave you two to freshen up. Supper is ready when you are."

"Thank you, ma'am."

Hattie was too amazed at how she was being treated to respond politely. Iris shut the door so she could put on fresh clothes before going to eat. She removed her hat and veil as well as the wig.

"I'm not going to wear the wigs here, because I would have to use the same one all the time. I think it's safe to use my own hair now. Once I change, I would like for you to braid it for me," she told Hattie.

"Yes, ma'am. Should I change too?"

"Yes. I think it would be a good idea. Put on your best dress, Hattie." Iris spoke quietly, not wanting anyone to hear her using a different name.

Ten minutes later, the two females emerged from their shared room clean and refreshed. Iris donned a respectable pastel dress lined with ruffles. Her hair spiraled around her head in a silky black braid. Hattie wore her best black uniform dress with white collar and apron.

Tom stood from his chair in the parlor as the women emerged. "Right this way," he told them.

Missus Sellers had already filled five bowls with steaming beef stew. A plateful of raisin muffins sat in the middle of the table, waiting to be devoured as well.

"Please, come sit down," the senior Sellers told everyone from the head of the table. "Mary Grace, you join us now, you may sit beside me if you like," he told the colored woman. He did not approve of slavery, and he knew this woman was just that.

Hattie looked toward Iris for approval. Iris' eyes were large with uncertainly. Back home, slaves never sat at the dining table with their masters. Hattie was her friend, but still … However, they were in the north now, she realized. Things were different here. Knowing that this was their only shelter, Iris decided to play along. She barely nodded approval.

"Yes sir," Hattie responded to the elder man. She took a seat on the bench nearest his end of the table. Iris took her place beside Hattie. Missus Sellers took the other end of the table while Tom sat on the bench opposite the two women. This was going to be an interesting meal.

Tom and his parents joined hands. His parents then held out their other hands to hold Iris' and Hattie's hands. Hattie timidly complied. Once the circle was complete, Mister Sellers began a prayer of thanksgiving to God. He thanked God for bringing his son back for a visit, for his lovely wife, for their abundance, for their guests' safe travel, and for the future. He also asked for quick healing for a Mister Greenwood who had recently broken his leg. At the end, he thanked God for their food and said "Amen."

"Amen," the family echoed.

Hattie sat in her chair dismayed at being included in the prayer and the supper. Everyone else began eating.

"Mary Grace, are you ill?" Missus Sellers asked.

Blinking out of her shock, Hattie answered, "No, ma'am. I'm fine. Just fine."

The woman smiled. "Good."

Dinner was pleasant enough as conversation was kept fairly light. Tom's parents wanted to know where their guests were from and under what circumstances they had arrived in Williamsport. Iris repeated her lies.

"Oh my dear ... What you must have been through," Missus Sellers sympathized. "I am so sorry."

"Thank you. I will just be thankful to get into a home again and get settled down," Iris professed. At least this part was the truth.

Senior Mister Sellers cleared his throat. He looked toward his son. "You know Tom, the old Myers place is up for sale. A bit run down, but ... available."

"That house gives me the creeps," Tom told his father. He looked at Iris. "Missus Myers killed her husband there several years ago. She was later tried, found guilty and hanged."

Hattie let out a noise. Iris looked at her with warning eyes. She then looked at Tom. "Regardless, I would still like to see it. If nobody has wanted it in several years, I might get a good price on it."

"That you would," the older man answered with a laugh.

Missus Sellers cleared her throat and looked at her husband. "Dear, you know what they say." She then turned to Iris. "I don't think it would be a good choice for you, Missus Blackheart."

"Why not, ma'am?"

"Well ... I don't want to scare you dear. But they say that, um, well ... that Mister Myers' ghost still visits from time to time."

Hattie let out another noise. "No ghosts, ma'am. No ghosts!" she pleaded.

"Very well, but I don't believe in them," Iris stated for the record. "Are there any other homes available?"

"Only one that I can think of, and it's way out of town," Mister Sellers spoke. "But don't give up, dear. We can ask around at church on Sunday."

4

Two days later, Hattie and Iris joined the Sellers trio in church. Apparently, Mister Sellers had been the minister in the community for years, but had recently stepped down. A younger minister, Orville Shepherd, probably in his mid to late thirties, now took the pulpit. His wife, Tina Louise and four children, all boys, sat in the first pew. Iris noted about fifty people in the church house. It was located just near the river running south of town.

In the past two days, she had made friends with the good family. She learned that thirty year old Tom was a captain in the military and lived in a camp outside of Harrisburg. He was able to come home occasionally to visit. He had never been married, much to his mother's dismay. His older brother, Wayne and his wife and four children, lived in Scranton, about seventy miles away. They came home twice a year. Both parents, Betsy and Gerald, were wonderfully kind. Iris thought that Gerald Sellers was being overly gratuitous to Hattie, practically waiting on her hand and foot. It was very odd behavior.

Tom had slept in the loft these last two nights since his old room was taken. He was intrigued by this woman and her slave-servant. There was a mystery about her that made him interested. He wanted to find out more of this raven haired beauty and her real story. She was kind, and obviously well bred, but he just knew there was something she was holding back. He would get to the truth in time.

After church, Gerald introduced his house guests to the towns-folk. He even inquired as to property that Missus Blackheart might purchase. There was only one suggestion made. The Myers' house.

"Mister Sellers, would you be willing to show me the Myers' house anyway?" Iris asked during the drive home.

"If you're sure, I'll take you," he agreed.

"It won't hurt to look," she told him. "Besides, I've no other choice."

"We can go this afternoon, after dinner if you want to," he decided.

Iris agreed. Why not? It was a fine day.

After lunch, Hattie and Betsy were swapping recipes. Iris had not told her servant what she was up to. She knew Hattie would be vexed at the thought of living in a ghost house. Expecting to go with Gerald Sellers, Iris was disappointed to find him asleep in his chair by the fire within minutes after eating.

"He does this every Sunday," Tom whispered. "He will sleep for two hours exactly."

Iris' face pouted.

"What's wrong?" the well-groomed soldier asked.

"Your father was going to show me the Myers' place this after-noon. I guess it will just have to wait," she answered.

"I can take you," he offered eagerly.

"Would you?" Iris caught herself showing too much eagerness and appreciation. She did not want to give this man the wrong idea. "I mean, that would be very kind, thank you," she answered in a more normal voice.

"I'll hitch up the team. Ma, I'm taking Missus Blackheart for a drive. Be back in a while."

Once outside, he offered information. "This place is just north of town. Not too far from everything, maybe three fourths of a mile. It's set up on the side of a hill."

"How big is it?" Iris asked as she climbed into the seat.

"I've never actually been inside. But it looks big enough from the road," he answered honestly.

Tom climbed up and flicked the reins.

As the horses moved, Iris asked, "How did Missus Myers kill her husband?"

"They say she ran him through with a fire poker. Can you imagine? What on earth could have made her so crazy as to go and do something like that?" he asked.

Iris knew all too well why a wife might want to kill her husband. She remained silent for a moment before asking, "Why did she do it?"

"Who knows? Some say she was getting even for something he'd done. Thing is, nobody knows what he did."

"What did she say at the trial?"

"She said it was self-defense, that he was hurting her, but nobody believed her. We all knew him and we never saw him hurt her. He was a nice man. He went to church and everything. The town hated to hang his wife, but the law is the law," he concluded.

Iris wiped away a small tear which had escaped from her eye. She turned away so Tom would not see and wonder. Her heart broke for this woman. Iris was glad her story would not turn out the same way. She was even more grateful now that she had left him back in Lexington. Her thoughts were drawn to the present when she noticed that the buggy was slowing down. Iris looked ahead. An older woman, dressed in homespun wool and wrapped in a shawl walked toward them.

Tom smiled. "Good afternoon, Missus Reed," he greeted politely.

Iris' mind perked up. Missus Reed? This was Samuel's grandmother.

"Afternoon, Mister Sellers. Good to see you again," she greeted in a sweet elderly voice.

"Missus Reed, this is Missus Blackheart. She's just moved here from Georgia. I'm taking her out to look at the Myers' place," he explained.

"Missus Blackheart," the elder woman acknowledged. "All the way from Georgia, you say? My, my!" The woman looked at Tom and smiled. Then she turned back to Iris. "What brings you here, dear?"

"My health, ma'am. I needed cooler air."

The old woman nodded her head. "So I hear it is unbearable hot down there. I've family in South Carolina myself you see. My son and grandson. My son was just here visiting earlier this month, but he's gone back home now." She paused. "Got any children Missus Blackheart?"

Iris quenched the little pain in her heart and pursed her lips together. "No, ma'am."

"Where's your husband, dear?" the lady innocently questioned.

"He passed away, ma'am, at sea this past winter." At least her story was solidifying. Once it was told and retold, the entire town would believe it.

"Oh, that's too bad. My husband passed away years ago, but I haven't quit looking for another. Neither should you. Mister Sellers here is a good catch," the lady said with a wink.

Iris laughed at the woman. She was sure full of questions and opinions.

Tom coughed. "Missus Reed, when are you going to stop trying to set me up with a wife? You know I don't want to be tied down. I'm still holding out for you!" he teased.

"Oh go on now," the grandmother giggled. "Missus Blackheart, it was nice to meet you."

Iris nodded.

"Good day, ma'am," Tom spoke before starting the team again.

Missus Reed resumed her walk.

After going on a bit, Tom turned to Iris. "You'll have to excuse what she said. She's been trying to find me a wife for ten years now. Please don't feel threatened by me. Besides, I'm leaving in the morning and won't be back for another month."

"You are? Well, it's of no consequence anyway. I've no intentions of remarrying. Ever," she stated boldly.

This intrigued him. Most young women were anxious to marry. "Why not?" Tom asked.

"I have my reasons, sir. Are we close to the house yet?"

Tom ignored her. "Don't you want children? Every other woman I've ever met, your age, wants a husband and children." Mothers had been tossing their daughters at him since he was twenty. He was so tired of it.

Iris bit her lower lip until it hurt. She closed her eyes to fight back the memory of her unborn child. "No Mister Sellers, no children for me," she finally answered with as steady a voice as she could muster.

"Hmm," was all that he said.

They were in town now. Tom spoke greetings to a few people he knew before turning the buggy onto a small road that lead north from town. It meandered around a steep hill before opening up to more level ground.

"Where does this road go to?" Iris asked.

"There's a small village about fifteen miles north. If you keep following the road though, it will lead you all the way to New York state, to a town called Elmira."

"New York? Goodness!"

After half a mile more, Tom informed his passenger that the house was just ahead. Iris strained to see it. The white washed home was set back off the road, up against a hill. It was two stories, with a slender front porch. Several boards were missing, and the entire structure needed care. The glass window in the upper room was broken out. Leaves and limbs littered the yard from years of neglect. Tom pulled the wagon into the yard and offered his hand to Iris.

"Dare we go in?" she asked him.

"I guess we could," he answered.

"Who owns it now?"

Tom responded, "I think it went to Mister Myer's brother in Harrisburg. He's had it for sale ever since the funeral."

"Is it really haunted?" Iris questioned skeptically.

"I don't know," Tom answered, stepping onto the porch. The floorboards squeaked beneath his boots. A chill ran down his spine, but he didn't tell Missus Blackheart.

A thick layer of dust covered everything inside. All the furniture stood as it did the day of the murder. Tom and Iris carefully wandered around the first floor. There was a large kitchen, a parlor, one bedroom, and a closet beneath the stairs for storage.

"It's spooky in here," Tom confessed his fear.

"It's just unkempt," Iris assured him. "I'm going to look upstairs." She took the steps carefully, making sure the boards would hold her. She reached the top without incident. "There are four rooms up here," she called out to Tom.

"They say she killed him in their bedroom," Tom warned her. He came up the stairs too, warily.

Iris boldly opened each door in turn. One was undoubtedly the master bedroom, the other was tastefully done as a guest room. The third was set up as a nursery, and the fourth was used for storage. None of the rooms were remarkably large, but they would nicely suit her purpose as a boarding house.

"I'll take it," she declared to an astonished Tom at the top of the landing.

"Are you sure that's wise?" he questioned.

"Yes. I want to open a boarding house and this will be perfect," she told him.

"You're crazy!" he stated, turning to go back down the steps.

Iris questioned, "Do you know how I can get in touch with Mister Myers?"

Tom shook his head. "No, but my father will know. He will help you with everything."

And so it was done. Within a week, Iris and Hattie were setting up in their new home. Hattie was absolutely terrified about living in a supposedly haunted house. But Iris assured her that they would be safe, that it was just a house. Hattie took quarters in the room downstairs off the kitchen. Iris set herself up in the guest room upstairs. She would keep the master room open for paying guests. In time, she would set up the other two rooms for guests as well. For now, they had their work cut out for them. Everything had to be cleaned and dusted. The drapes, the linens, the furniture, the dishes, even the walls had a layer of dust. Plus, the window in the nursery had to be repaired and the boards on the front porch replace.

Late in the afternoon on the first day, Hattie had her hands in a large wash pot soaking all the curtains. She had spent her entire day in the kitchen cleaning every inch. All the dishes were on the counter waiting to be washed. All of a sudden, a bowl crashed behind her.

Hattie screamed in terror and ran out of the house as fast as she could through the back door. Iris left her spot in the parlor where she was sweeping and looked into the kitchen.

"What happened?" she asked out loud. Iris saw the broken pottery bowl on the floor and went through the open door to find her servant. "Hattie, what happened?" she repeated.

"There's a spirit in that house, ma'am. I ain't goin' back in there!"

"What happened with the bowl, Hattie?"

"It flew off the counter! All by itself!" Hattie answered in a panic.

"That's just impossible Hattie. Things just don't move by themselves. I'll go clean it up while you compose yourself, but I expect you to return to your chores in five minutes. I can't clean this place by myself," Iris scolded.

Hattie returned, but she was not happy. *"I could just leave,"* she thought to herself. *"I don't have to stay here. I'm in the north. I can be free."* But she didn't leave. She had no money and no place to go. Besides, she did like Iris, most of the time.

Iris had purchased food from the small store in town and had everything delivered to the house. When the goods arrived, she helped unload all the staples into the kitchen.

"I can't believe you bought this place," the store owner told her. "Grown men are scared of this house."

"Well Mister Harris, I am not," she told him curtly.

Hattie was out behind the house stringing a clothes line so she could hang her dripping linens. Her mind began to wander. How nice it would be if she could have a house of her own. And a husband too. She was the only colored person in town at the moment though, for she had not seen another in over a week. She was twenty after all, and a woman had dreams. She let out a sigh. Hattie was a little lonely for her own kind. She missed some of the other maids back home. She thought about what they might be doing. It had been two weeks now since they had left Lexington. She wondered what the master was doing too.

5

South Carolina

Johnathan Picket waited at the train depot. When Iris did not arrive, he grew alarmed. He went to the ticket man inside and inquired, "Where is my wife?"

"Sir, I'm sure I do not know," came the man's response.

"Her name is Missus Johnathan Picket. Was she on the train?"

"You can ask the conductor, Mister Picket," the man replied. He was much too busy to fret over a late arrival.

Johnathan ran to find the conductor before the train pulled out again. "Excuse me sir, was there a Missus Johnathan Picket on this train? She was supposed to arrive from Charleston today."

The conductor thought about it for a moment before answering. "Doesn't ring a bell," the older man replied. "But I've seen a lot of folks today."

"But ... she has to be here, she was due back today. She was traveling with her slave, Hattie. Both of them are twenty years old. My wife has coal black hair," Johnathan demanded.

"Sorry, sir. Nobody of that description boarded today. Least I didn't see them ..."

Johnathan wrung his hands together while he thought of his next action. He would send a telegraph to her parents in Charleston. Maybe they knew where she was, and if she had been delayed. He ran down to the telegraph office and sent an inquiry immediately.

"I will wait for an answer," he told the man behind the counter. The man, a very thin nervous sort of fellow, ticked away on his machine while Johnathan paced the floor.

Half an hour went by. No response.

"Send it again!" Johnathan demanded from the agent.

"Sir, I assure you, it went through the first time," the man said timidly. "It will cost to send it again."

"I don't care!" Mister Picket shouted. "Send it!"

"Very well sir …"

Another half an hour passed with still no reply. Johnathan was in a state now. He was furious! He stormed out of the telegraph office and marched back down to the depot.

"Give me a ticket for the next train to Charleston," he ordered, slamming money on the counter.

"It doesn't leave until morning, Mister Picket," the man told him.

Johnathan grabbed the ticket and sped back to his horse. He would go home, pack a small bag, then return on horseback in the morning.

That night, Johnathan Wayne Picket spent over two hours in his study drinking hard whiskey. Still no word from his wife or her parents. He was vexed, to say the least. Where was she? No word at all since she left. His mind began to wander. Had she met another man? He would kill her if it were so. He would kill the other man too. Morning could not come soon enough. He would find her!

At every stop along the route, Johnathan inquired as to his wife and her maid. Nobody had seen them. His anger grew. Finally in Charleston, he quickly made strides to her parents' home. He knocked heavily on the locked door. When the servant opened it, Johnathan pushed his way inside.

"Mister Payton, Missus Payton, where is Iris?" he demanded. He found Savannah working on some embroidery in the parlor. "Where is Iris?" he questioned again.

"I don't know," she replied, shaking in fright.

"She didn't come home on the train yesterday. I want to know where she is! Did you put her on the train?" he asked in a sinister voice.

"I, I ..." Savannah didn't quite know how to answer.

"No, we didn't," Tom answered, pointing a gun in Johnathan's direction. "Now you back up from my wife before I end your miserable life."

Johnathan cocked an eyebrow, but backed away from his mother-in-law. "Now see here Tom, I don't mean no harm. I just want my wife."

"She's gone, Johnathan. We don't know where she went. She wouldn't even tell us. Only that she was leaving you because you beat her and even made her lose a child. You are wicked and evil, and we never want to see you again," Tom threatened. He steadied the gun and took aim at Johnathan's chest. "Go back home and forget about her."

Johnathan chucked darkly, then slowly walked over toward his father-in-law. "This ain't the end of this," he growled.

Tom cocked the gun. "Don't ever show your face here again or I'll blow it off!"

Johnathan stood tall as he left the room. He walked toward town in a sort of stupor. She had left him. He never thought she would have had it in her. Where could she have gone? Did she have friends or relatives out of town? None that he knew of, except in Charleston. He decided to stay in town for a while and do some snooping around. She couldn't be far. She wasn't brave enough to leave her parents.

Johnathan headed for the nearest hotel to get a room for the night. After registering, he would go to the sheriff's office and report that his wife was missing. He would give them a description, and one at the train depot as well, just in case.

Mister Picket grew more flustered by the hour. He remained in Charleston for two days without any leads. He asked around everywhere for information, but nobody could help him. He decided to place an ad in the paper.

"How long she been gone?" the clerk at the paper asked.

"Two and a half weeks now."

"Wow! That long? She could be anywhere with that much time. Have you placed ads in other newspapers?" the man wondered.

"No. Think I should?"

"If my wife were missing, I would," the clerk replied.

"Very well. How do I go about doing that from here?" Johnathan asked.

"I can do it for you. We newspapers work together on some stories. I can get this one out. I suggest Atlanta, Savannah, Wilmington, Columbia and Raleigh."

"We live just outside Columbia," Johnathan explained. "Someone would have seen and recognized her there. Do the other cities though."

The young man at the desk nodded, then added, "Have you been down to the docks Mister Picket? Passengers go in and out of there every day too."

"I'll go now. I'm at the Hampton Hotel if you hear anything. Please let me know immediately."

The man agreed, thinking that he was doing a noble deed in helping to find a missing wife. How very exciting the mystery was. It would certainly help to sell papers. It was a story the people would be interested in.

Down at the docks, Johnathan made inquiries. He was informed that too many people came through there every day to possibly remember one woman and her maid. Dozens of women and their maids had boarded ships over the last few weeks.

"May I see records then, possibly?" he asked.

"That's up to each captain, sir," he was told.

"You aren't being very helpful," he growled at the dock man.

"Sorry sir, it's the best I can do. I don't have individual records of these things. Only the captains do. We see about fifteen passenger ships through here each week."

Johnathan slapped his hat on a pole in frustration. Then he set out to speak with each of the captains now docked.

Two hours later, an angry Johnathan returned to the hotel. He'd gotten nowhere. Of the three ships in port, only two captains allowed him to review their passenger lists. Iris' name was not on them, nor any names that sounded familiar. Maybe she had taken the train out after all. Maybe she had gone west, to Alabama, or Mississippi. Possibly even as far as Louisiana. Johnathan kicked the bed post. He'd reached a dead end.

After four more days in town and no word from any of the newspapers, Johnathan decided to return home. He left his name and information with a dozen people, just in case.

Once he reached home, Johnathan immediately went into his liquor cabinet. After downing a few swigs of his strongest whiskey, he took a pistol and walked out to the barn. All of his slaves steered clear, knowing their master was in a horrid mood. Everyone heard the single shot fired in the barn. They waited a few silent moments before looking to see what had happened. The bravest of the men began to walk toward the building, but all jumped out of the way as Johnathan entered the doorway. He stormed back to the grand house. Once he was gone, they entered the barn. Their master had shot Missus Picket's favorite horse between the eyes. They all wondered why.

April 13, 1861

A week later, back in Williamsport, Hattie and Iris were just about done with the inside of their new home. No further incidents had occurred to frighten Hattie and she was becoming more comfortable with her surroundings. Everything had been cleaned and the house was actually looking nice. Mister Harris had helped

replace the broken boards on the porch and the broken window.
The widow, Missus Reed, had brought flower bulbs for Iris to plant
out front. Mister and Missus Sellers had offered some seeds for her
to plant in the garden. Everyone was being so considerate. Iris had
made new friends at church too, so it was fairly easy during the day
to be happy and forget her bad memories.

That is, until late in the afternoon on April thirteenth. Missus
Reed came walking up the road in a hurry. "Missus Blackheart,"
she called out.

Iris heard her from the upstairs window and stuck out her
head. "Hello, Missus Reed. Come on in."

"Have you heard?" the older woman asked in a huff.

"Heard what, ma'am?"

"Oh, my dear! Pray for my son and grandson, they are in
peril," she gasped out.

"Whatever is the matter?"

"Charleston is under attack! The Union Navy fired upon the
fort yesterday. They attacked all day and night. The north and south
are at war!" she finished dramatically.

Iris went pale. Feeling faint, she leaned against the doorway.
"How do you know this?" Iris asked in a far away voice.

"It was in the Harrisburg paper. News of it came on the train
today. It's just so awful. If my men join the military, they could be
killed. Pray, pray!" she begged.

"Was it just the fort, or the whole town too?" Iris wondered,
panicked at the thought of her parents in danger.

"I think just the fort for now," the woman replied. "But who
knows where this war will go. If they take Charleston, they can go
inland, to where my boys are. Oh, I just don't know what to do."

Iris slept fitfully that night, tossing and turning with night-
mares. She contemplated the thought of writing to her mother a
letter to make sure she was safe. But then, Johnathan would be able
to find her. She couldn't risk it. Although, if the north and south
were truly at war, then the borders would close and he would have
a hard time getting to her. But her letter would have a hard time

reaching her mother. And if the northern officers found out she was a southerner, they might send her back, and then what would she do? Or worse, they might put her in jail as a prisoner. All these crazy thoughts ran wild through her mind until Iris wanted to scream. Sometime, around four in the morning, she got out of bed to fix herself a cup of tea. Maybe it would help calm her nerves and let her sleep.

Hattie peeked out her door, fully expecting some glowing apparition in the kitchen.

"It's just me, Hattie," Iris spoke softly.

"I's so glad, ma'am. I was scared to open my door," she confessed.

"I can't sleep. I keep thinking about Mother and Tom. I'm scared for them. I'm scared to be here too, in the north. If we are truly at war, these people may turn against me."

"Can't be worse than the master, ma'am," Hattie spoke wisely.

Iris nodded. "You're right, Hattie. I'm worrying over things that haven't happened. I'm sure Mother and Tom have enough sense to get out of harm's way." Hattie sipped her hot drink. "Want some tea?"

"No, ma'am. I want sleep. Goodnight." Hattie returned to bed and the house remained quiet until dawn.

6

Summer 1862

The following year, news of the war filtered into Williamsport through newspapers from Harrisburg, Philadelphia, New York and Pittsburgh. It was a trying time for everyone. Iris' boarding house had established itself and had respectable returns. Tom Sellers had gone off to battle, writing home to his parents from time to time to keep them abreast of events. Betsy worried for her son, but kept up a good spirit of faith about her. Iris wondered occasionally if Johnathan was off fighting too, and if he were alive or dead. For all she knew, she could be a widow now. Regardless, she was not interested in men at all. Several had tried to capture her attention in the last twelve months, but Iris turned them all down as politely as possible. As far as she knew, she was still married, and bound by vows made to God. She would not dream of jeopardizing her eternal soul by courting with or marrying another man.

Life carried on pleasantly enough for Iris. The season had come and gone over the past year. She and Hattie had seen snow like never before. The winter here was harsh, but they had survived it just fine. This year, spring had come with an array of beautiful flowers in her new garden. And the vegetables were now coming out nicely. It was a comfortably warm summer and the days were long and quiet. Thankfully, the war was far away.

Iris had become quite aware of the issue over slavery in the last year as well. She knew this entire war mess came from that great political issue. She wondered if Hattie ever felt like she was still in great bondage. Her life had much more leisure and freedom to it now than ever before. She would have to make a point to ask Hattie about it someday.

One hot August afternoon, Iris and Hattie rocked on their front porch. Only one room was rented and the man was working in town, so there was very little to do. Hattie hummed a little tune while Iris just closed her eyes and enjoyed the peace. She felt secure in her little world now. It was wonderful.

"Hattie, do you ever feel like I mistreat you?" Iris asked, knowing they were alone.

"Ma'am?" Hattie asked, taken by surprise.

"Do you ever feel mistreated? Do you feel like a downtrodden slave?" Iris clarified.

"Um … how da I answer that, ma'am?" Hattie asked, fearful that her real answer might cause problems.

Iris opened her eyes and looked at her maid with exasperation. "With truth, Hattie. How do you feel about it?"

Hattie bit on her lips for a few seconds, then was brave enough to answer, "I'd like my freedom, ma'am."

Iris' heart hammered in her chest. The thought of losing Hattie frightened her. "You'd leave me? All alone here?" she asked in astonishment.

Hattie couldn't look her mistress in the eye. "If I was going to do that, I'd a done it already," she replied flatly. "I'd just like to be freed. Like you felt when you left the master," she explained.

"Hmmm," Iris answered, deep in thought. "I will think on it, Hattie."

There was silence for nearly ten minutes as the women continued their rocking. It was broken however by someone whistling down the road.

"Do ya hear that?" Hattie whispered. She was still cautious for possible ghosts.

"Yes, I do. Must be someone coming."

Both women looked down the road to see who was coming up the lane. After a moment, they both saw a colored man walking with a lively spirit in his step. He wore clean clothes and a hat and carried a knapsack on a stick.

"My, my!" Hattie whispered. This was only the fifth colored person she had seen in over a year. She watched carefully as he came near.

When the man entered the yard, Iris stood up on the porch. The man removed his hat and took a bow before her. "At your service, Madam," he called out formally. "Barney's my name. Barney Montgomery."

"Mister Montgomery," she replied with a nod. He was a young man, in his twenties. "What can I do for you?"

"Well, ma'am, I was told you might have work for me. I travel around doing odd jobs where I'm needed. Might I be of service to you?" he asked.

"Do you have references?" Iris asked.

"Yes, ma'am. In my bag here," he answered, pulling it off his shoulder. He opened the cloth and pulled out some papers. He then walked to the porch and handed them over.

Iris read them carefully. "I might be able to use you, Mister Montgomery. Our outhouse needs some repair, as does the well. And our yard needs some work. I'll pay you twenty-five cents a day, plus meals. You can sleep in the shed out back."

"Thank you, ma'am, thank you kindly," he said grinning. "What do you want done first?"

"The outhouse."

"I'll get right on it."

He replaced his hat and tipped it toward Hattie. Hattie blushed, thankful she was in the shade and darkly skinned. From the corner of her eye, however, she watched as the young man walked around to the side of the house.

"I saw that," Iris teased.

Hattie scoffed. "You saw nothin'!"

Iris sat back down in her chair. "It will be nice to have those repairs made," she spoke out loud. "Is there enough dinner for one more?"

"Yes'm. There's enough. A whole chicken, mashed potatoes, green beans and cornbread," Hattie replied.

"Sounds good. I'm sure we'll find out more of this Mister Montgomery at dinner."

The dining room in the boarding house held two tables. That left enough room for everyone. When Hattie was making final preparations for supper, Iris asked her, "Do you want to sit alone tonight with Barney?"

"No, ma'am," Hattie answered. She had never been around colored men much. She had always been a house servant, and there were only so many colored men who worked in a house. Usually, the butler and one man servant or a foot man or two. And never in her experience, were these men young and interesting. Just the thought of sitting next to him gave Hattie butterflies in her stomach.

At six o'clock, their border, Mister Graham, returned from his work in town. He was doing something for the Union Army, but never did quite go into details. Promptly at six-thirty, Hattie called supper. Barney had washed and changed into clean clothing. He knocked on the back door timidly. "Come on in, Mister Montgomery," Hattie called out.

He politely wiped his shoes before entering. He stood inside the doorway, awaiting his plate. He planned to take it out back and eat in the pleasant hours of the evening.

"Come sit down," Hattie spoke shyly. He gave her a strange look. She gave him a reassuring nod. He walked over to the first table, closest to the kitchen. "No, here," she corrected, tapping on the one table set for four.

"I don't understand," he confessed respectfully. "Shouldn't I take my plate and go out back?"

"No, Mister Montgomery, we all sit down together," Iris told him as she entered the room.

Mister Graham was behind her. Iris introduced him to her new hired help. "He will be joining us at the table tonight."

Unheard of! Barney's mind tried to grasp this new idea. Everyone sat down with Iris and Mister Graham at the head of the table, and both Hattie and Barney on opposite sides. Hattie's stomach fluttered nervously, but she wasn't sure why.

"Mister Graham, will you do us the honor?" Iris asked.

Barney watched as the other three bowed their heads to pray. The man's prayer was kind and simple. Although his eyes were open, Barney answered with an "Amen."

All four at the table helped themselves to the food of their choice. It was obvious that Barney was very uncomfortable sitting at the table with the white folks. Iris nearly felt sorry for him. So did Hattie.

"Where are you from?" she asked timidly.

"Alabama," he answered after swallowing a big bite of mashed potatoes. "Just south of Montgomery. That's how I got my last name," he told them with a little smile.

"You're far from home, young man," Mister Graham told him. "What brings you way up here?"

Barney eagerly took a piece of cornbread and put it on his plate. "Freedom sir," he answered simply.

Hattie smiled at this. She understood. She liked this man. He was attractive too. He was muscular with short hair and a nice grin.

"We're from ..." Hattie began.

Iris cleared her throat suddenly to interrupt her maid before any secrets came out.

"Georgia," Hattie fibbed, glad that Iris had caught it in time.

"Never been there. Went straight north when I left," he informed them.

"How long have you been gone?" Hattie wondered.

He swallowed his bite of cornbread. This food was good. "Two years now."

Iris assumed he had been a runaway. He was lucky not to have been caught. Masters did terrible things to slaves who ran away and were caught. She tried not to think about it. Instead, she asked her border a question about his work to distract their minds.

Toward the end of supper, Barney leaned forward toward the young woman sitting across from him. She had a comely face and pretty eyes. "What's your name?" he whispered.

Hattie blushed again and smiled. "Mary Grace is what people call me," she answered honestly.

"Mary Grace, you cooked a fine supper. I thank you for it, and for your company."

Hattie blushed more, not knowing how to respond.

Iris saw what was happening and decided to rescue her poor maid. "Mister Montgomery," she called out.

Barney sat up quickly in his chair. "Yes, ma'am?"

"How's it coming on the outhouse?"

He let out a silent sigh of relief. He wasn't in trouble after all. "Coming along fine. I got several boards nailed back in place, but I could use some new planks for the roof and the seat."

"I have an account at the store in town. You may get some more wood tomorrow. Tell them you are working for me," Iris told him.

"Yes, ma'am."

"Do you need any tools?"

"A saw would be handy, ma'am. I have my own hammer and a few more nails left," he answered honestly.

"You just get what you need, but only what you need," she told him.

"Yes, ma'am. Thank you, ma'am. I'll have the outhouse fixed tomorrow."

"Shall we go enjoy the evening on the porch?" Mister Graham suggested.

"That would be pleasant, yes," Iris agreed. She did not feel threatened by this man, for he was in his forties and certainly too old for anything but friendship.

Hattie was left to the dishes before her evening chores were over.

"Want help?" Barney offered. "You can get it done in half the time."

Without a word, she nodded acceptance of this wonderful of-fer. "Is your missus always that pleasant to colored folk?" he asked. "I ain't never sat at the table with them before."

"Ever since coming here she has. Mister Sellers told her that we was all the same in God's eyes. So she started letting me sit with her at meals," Hattie answered.

Barney lowered his voice and leaned in closer. "You still her slave?"

Hattie nodded slowly.

"You could run away, like me. You's in the north now," he whispered.

"I know that," Hattie told him defensively. "I just ain't ready for that. Got no money and no place to go. Here, I got it good."

"But you ain't free," he said, looking her in the eye.

Hattie was riled by his words. "You go on now. Go outside!" she ordered.

"Join me when you're done?" he suggested.

Hattie narrowed her eyes. "Maybe."

Barney went out the back door whistling. Hattie could hear him the entire time she cleaned the supper dishes. It grated her nerves. When she was through, she went to her room for a while, trying to ignore him. After fifteen minutes though, she couldn't stand it any longer. She went out back to find him.

Barney was over near the well, looking down into the black pit. "This thing's all broken down," he informed her.

"I know that," she told him, hands on hips.

"The crank's broke," he stated. "How do you get water?"

Hattie motioned with her arms, "Lift up on the rope."

"That's too much work," he determined. Then he looked at her squarely. "You're pretty. How old are you?"

Hattie's frustrations were held back by his statement. It was the first compliment she had ever gotten from a man. Her mind scrambled.

"Mary Grace, how old are you?" he asked again, seeing her stupor.

"How old are you?" she asked in return.

He shrugged. "Don't know really. Best I can figure, about twenty-six or twenty-seven."

"I'm twenty and one," she confessed. "Did you run away from your master?"

He nodded. "Yes. Had to."

"He beat you?"

"Yeah. I took care of his horses. Every time he lost a race, he blamed it on me and let me know it," Barney answered soberly.

Hattie thought about that for a minute. "I'm glad you got free."

"Yeah. Me too. Want to take a walk?" he asked, changing the subject.

Barney and Hattie walked until dusk, talking about their lives and the mountainside.

"I sure never thought I'd see a mountain," Barney stated.

"Me neither. They sure is pretty though," Hattie observed. "You plan to stay in town long?"

"As long as the work lasts," he replied gently.

They walked on in silence while the lightning bugs glowed like yellow stars in the trees about them. Iris saw that Hattie and this man were beginning a friendship. She wondered what to do about it. She would have to give it some thought overnight.

The next several days were filled with joy for Hattie. She had taken to singing while she worked, which was unusual. At night, she and Barney took a short walk down the road, talking, laughing. They shared stories for endless hours. She knew she was falling in love and desperately wanted to spend all of her time with him. Hattie wondered if he felt the same way. Sure, he liked her, but was it more than that?

One day, while she was cleaning a room with Iris upstairs, Hattie got up the nerve to ask about love. "Ma'am, how d'ya know that you's in love?"

Iris grinned. "Well, you get this warm feeling inside, just when you're near that person," Iris explained. "You want to be with them all the time." Iris knew why her maid was asking. She had seen the pair together these last few days and was a little concerned about it. Maybe Mister Sellers could offer her some advice. Iris looked out the window at her hired man. "You thinking you're in love with Mister Montgomery?" she asked her maid.

Hattie just shrugged, not willing to admit to anything.

Barney had taken off his shirt while he worked on the well. It was a very hot day and he was working in the sun. Iris noticed the scars across his back.

"Hattie, take a look at that," she whispered. "Look at his back."

"Yes, ma'am. I know. He told me that his master used to whip him when his horse didn't win a race," Hattie explained.

Iris grimaced. How awful! How cruel! Iris said no more after that.

The next day however, she did pay a visit to Mister Sellers to ask his advice.

"I fear Mary Grace is falling in love with this man and that she will run away with him when his work is through," Iris confessed. "What can I do about it? I need Mary Grace."

The elder man thought about the situation for a moment before speaking.

"Do you feel that this Mister Montgomery fellow will take Mary Grace with him? Does he truly care for her?"

"I haven't come out and asked him, but they do spend every extra moment together," she answered.

"I see. First though, you need to know his intentions. Are they honorable? Is this just a friendship, or more than that? Then, if it is more, I would suggest that you gain a hand instead of losing one," he finished.

"What do you mean?"

The man smiled and explained. "I mean, take him on. Let him stay with you permanent. There's enough work to do at your house and a hired man could be very helpful. That way, if he and Mary Grace want to stay together, they can, and she won't leave you."

"Oh."

"And you should give Mary Grace her freedom," the man added.

"But she might leave," Iris told him with fear.

"That's true. She might. But nobody leaves a place where they are happy. Don't you agree?"

Iris bit her lip on that statement. He was right. She knew that firsthand. "Thank you Mister Sellers. Your advice is good, as always."

"Good day to you then, Missus Blackheart. And I hope to hear a report from you on Sunday."

Iris nodded before she left his home. With a sigh, she began the walk home. She had a task to do and it scared her a little.

That afternoon, while Hattie was busy preparing supper, Iris confronted Barney out in the yard.

"I would like a word with you, Mister Montgomery," she told him frankly.

"Yes, ma'am?"

"This friendship you have going with Mary Grace, I need to know if it's just a friendship, or something more than that."

Barney looked a little afraid. He backed up a step. "I haven't touched her, ma'am. I promise."

"I know that. Your behavior here has been honorable since the day you came. I was just wondering if you had feelings for her beyond friendship," she explained.

Barney looked at his new employer with suspicion. He wondered how to answer her question. Yes, he did like Mary Grace, very much. But he never stayed in one place long enough to get serious with any woman.

Iris watched as he thought about his response. There was an awkward moment of silence before she said, "You can tell the truth.

I won't get angry, regardless of your answer. I am merely looking out for my maid's best interest."

"Well, ma'am," he gulped. "I am fond of her. She's pretty. But I don't stay long enough in any place to go further than that."

Iris smiled. She could remedy that, and keep her maid as well. "How would you like to stay on here, permanent, and work for me all the time?" she asked.

Barney smiled big, then forced a more serious face. "I'd have to think on it, ma'am, if you don't mind."

"Certainly. Just let me know."

Later that night, after Hattie returned from her walk and Barney was settled down in his shed, Iris pulled Hattie aside to tell her something important. "Listen, I invited Mister Montgomery to stay on here permanent today. He told me he would think on it."

Hattie choked back tears. "Ma'am, I'm so glad. I didn't want him to go next week. I like him. I like him a lot."

"Do you think he likes you that much too?"

Hattie shrugged. "Don't know. Never done this before."

"Has he said anything?"

Hattie shook her head. "No, ma'am. Tonight he was real quiet on our walk. He usually talks a lot. Maybe he don't like me no more."

"He's got a lot on his mind Hattie. I wouldn't worry about it. I bet he'll be himself in a day or two."

The next morning came and went as usual. Barney came inside for breakfast, then left to go work in the yard. He had finished repairs to the outhouse and to the well. Both were in fine working order now. Iris left the house late in the morning to visit some friends. Around noon, Barney showed up at the back door with a bunch of wildflowers in his hand.

"For you, Mary Grace," he told her, holding them up.

Hattie smiled sweetly. "Thanks Barney," she told him. "Nobody's ever give me flowers before."

"When you take a break today, come see me?" he suggested questioningly.

"I will."

He then turned and left to do more work. About one o'clock, Hattie had time for a few minutes off. She went into the yard to find Barney cleaning up an old flower bed.

"I got some time now," she told him.

"Want to take a short walk?" he asked.

Hattie nodded. He led them into the woods, for privacy. "You know your lady came to me yesterday," he stated. "She offered me work to stay on permanent like."

"Yes, she told me," Hattie answered truthfully.

"She did?"

Hattie nodded.

"What else did she say?" he wondered curiously.

"Nothin' really. That you was going to think about it."

Barney was silent for a minute before asking, "Did she tell you I usually don't stay in one place for too long?"

Hattie's heart crashed. "No. You don't?" Her face fell in disappointment.

"That's what I wanted to talk to you about. See, I don't know what to tell her. No one ever offered me a job permanent before," he confessed.

"You like it here?" Hattie asked with the slightest hope.

"Yeah. She treats me real good."

"Then stay," she suggested.

Barney grinned. "Can we keep going on our walks at night?"

Hattie giggled. "Sure. She don't mind that. I don't neither," she confessed shyly.

They walked on in silence for several minutes. Barney cleared his throat. "You know, she asked me what my intentions were."

"Intentions for what? Leaving?" Hattie asked, truly innocent.

Barney shook his head. "No. For you."

Hattie's eyes grew wide with embarrassment. Her hand came up to cover her mouth as it dropped open. She held her breath for several seconds before letting it out slowly. "What did you say?" she asked in a whisper.

"Told her I was fond of you," he admitted honestly.

Hattie smiled. "I like you too."

One month later, on a comfortable September afternoon, Hattie and Barney Montgomery were married in a simple outdoor ceremony after Sunday church services. Hattie giggled with delight the entire time. Several of Iris' closest friends were in attendance, as were both the new and old ministers and their wives. Mister Montgomery seemed quite pleased with himself, smiling at everyone and shaking hands. He had become quite a likeable character in town. He worked hard and was a man of his word.

After the brief ceremony, everyone enjoyed a wonderful picnic of delicious food. No one enjoyed it more than Hattie however, for Iris had given her two whole days off as part of her wedding present. She had also presented her with papers of freedom. Hattie had cried for hours with joy the night before. She was free! Iris would now be paying her a monthly wage of five dollars, as she did for Mister Montgomery. Between the two of them, ten dollars a month was a fortune.

That night, Barney moved his things out of the shed and into Hattie's little room. They excused themselves early to retire. Iris knew what was in store, and had prepared Hattie as best she could. These thoughts brought back memories of Johnathan. Bad ones. Iris had to shake her head to get the thoughts out. No more men for her, ever!

Much to Iris' dismay the next morning, Hattie was up cooking breakfast around eight o'clock. She hummed a happy tune while she worked.

"You're happy today," Iris observed.

Hattie giggled. "Yes'm." She giggled again.

Iris was confused. "What will you do with your day off?"

"Don't know, ma'am," she answered with yet another giggle. Iris watched as Hattie finished her work and took two plates plus cups on a tray into her room. Once the door was closed, Iris could hear her giggling again.

"Good heavens!" Iris muttered under her breath. She returned her attention to the dress she was mending. "What could possibly be so much fun?"

7

September, 1864

Two years passed by as Iris hid away in her happy home in the Allegheny Mountains. The war raged on both in the North and in the South, coming into Pennsylvania in sixty-three. At the battle of Gettysburg, many men lost their lives, including Captain Tom Sellers. It had been an awful blow to his parents. Iris worried for her stepfather's safety. Iris wondered if he was in the war. She also wondered if her mother was safe. On occasion, she also considered her husband. She wondered if he were alive or dead. Iris wondered how the war would change things. How would life be different when it was over? Could she ever go back home? What would the Yankees do if they defeated the South? What would the Confederacy do if they won? It was all so very, very troubling, not knowing the future.

"Barney?" Iris called out for her hired hand as he tended the garden.

"Yes, ma'am?" he replied respectfully. Noah, Barney's fifteen month old son, looked up from behind a pumpkin.

"I'd like you to run an errand for me, please."

Barney brushed the dirt from his hands and gathered his only son. He held him sideways behind his back while the boy grinned happily.

Iris continued her instructions. "Please go down to the train station and leave word that I want a recent paper from Harrisburg. Also, get me the South's listings of all those missing in action, captured, wounded or killed in battle. Tell them I want Confederate listings as I have kin down there and I'm concerned about them."

Barney furrowed his brows. "You sure that's wise, ma'am?" he questioned.

Iris shut her eyes. "Just go. I'm worried about my parents and need some news from home. Please Barney, just go."

"Yes, ma'am. Can you tell Mary Grace where I've gone?" Barney swung his beloved little son in front of his chest and off they went toward town.

Iris went back inside to find Hattie. The colored woman was resting in her room with her three month old daughter. "Hattie?" Iris whispered.

"Yes? I'm awake."

Iris opened the door. "I just sent Barney on an errand into town. He won't be long."

Hattie opened her eyes and smiled with a nod. She was exhausted. This second baby had been hard on her health and the delivery had been especially difficult. To make matters worse, the baby was colicky and cried every night. It had gotten to the point where their house guests were complaining. Iris knew if something wasn't done, she would be out of business. It had come time for the Montgomery family to have their own place. She planned to make inquiries. They could certainly build a cabin on the other side of the property where her house stood. She would seek Mister Seller's advice on how to go about it all. In the last three years, he had become her surrogate father, stepping in with advice and help whenever it was needed. She was thankful for him.

One week later, Iris had her newspaper from Harrisburg and her listings from the Confederate military. She was much relieved to find her stepfather was listed only as wounded. Her husband was not listed at all. She did recognize dozens of names of men and boys she had known since childhood. It was heart wrenching to think of all those lives lost.

That very same day, Iris welcomed a new border to her home. It was a Union soldier by the name of David Stoneman. She guessed him to be in his late twenties with curly brown hair. He immediately began to ask questions.

"So, what brings you to the north? I hear you're the local southern belle," he stated while they chatted in the parlor.

"Yes. I'm from Georgia."

"Where abouts?" he asked curiously.

"Oh, it's a little place. I doubt you've ever heard of it," she answered, trying to put him off. She did not like all these questions.

"Try me. I know a lot about Southern geography."

Iris took a breath and tried to think of a place she had heard of. "It's called Gordon," she told him.

"Never heard of it," he answered, sizing up his suspect. Lieutenant David Stoneman had his assignment. He had to find out more of this Southern woman. The Union Army had heard of her request for Southern casualty lists, and decided it was worth checking out. They had no room for southern sympathizers or spies in this area. She could be up to something. "Why did you move all the way up here?" he asked next.

Iris decided he was suspicious of her presence here and so turned on her charm. She smiled in cool southern way. "Why Lieutenanant Stoneman, for my health, of course. My doctor told me that the heat was bad for my breathing, so I had to move to a cool place. He was right too, I'm much healthier now." Hoping to change the subject, she asked, "And what about you? Where are you from, Lieutenant?"

David considered her question. It was too risky to give her viable information at this point, so he lied. "I'm from Philadelphia."

"That's nice. I've never been there. What's it like?"

His suspicion grew. Was she seeking out information to pass on to Southern contacts? "Let's change the subject," he suggested. "I still want to talk about you."

"But there's really not much more to say. I'm just me, end of story," she told him while growing angry at his insistence on facts about her life. She began to grow nervous too.

At that moment, Hattie walked in to call supper. Iris and the Lieutenant walked toward the table. He was her only border tonight, much to her disappointment. It would be just the two of them at the table, for Barney and Hattie had taken to eating later with their children.

"Would you care to say a prayer for the meal?" Iris suggested.

"Certainly Missus Blackheart," he readily agreed. "Dear Lord, help us to be thankful. Help us to be mindful of your commandments. Watch over our soldiers and keep them safe." David opened his eyes to see if his hostess was watching him. He was surprised to find her eyes shut tight. He continued, "Help us not to lie or be deceitful as it is a sin. Bless the food. Amen."

"Amen," Iris answered, trying to interpret his words. Did he mean something by them? Did he know something? Her heart quickened as she reached for her fork.

They both began to serve when the Lieutenant began his questions again. "So where is your husband?"

Iris tried not to show her annoyance. She pretended to be quite grieved. "He died three years ago, on our trip north. He became quite ill on the ship and went home to be with the Lord." Forgive me Lord for these necessary lies, she prayed silently.

"How long were you married?"

"A year and a half."

"No children?"

Iris shot him a warning glance. "Sir, that is not your business."

"Forgive me. What made you chose this town?" he asked instead.

Iris took a breath. "I saw it on a map once. It sounded nice." That was partially true.

"When your husband died, why didn't you go back home?"

"Like I said, I had to come north for my health." She was getting truly irritated now. This was not a pleasant conversation.

"Lieutenant, if you will, please stop this barrage of questions. I find it most unbecoming an officer and it is certainly not proper dinner behavior."

Not wanting to set her off further for the moment, David decided to stop. He had as long as he needed to get answers. And if he blew it on the first night, he would never get anywhere with this investigation. "Very well," he sighed. "What would you like to talk about?"

Iris thought for a moment. "Cabins. Do you know how to build them? My hired couple needs a new home."

The next morning, David spoke with Barney about how to build a cabin. He also asked questions about the mistress of the home. Barney answered as little as possible, not knowing if Missus Blackheart was in trouble of some kind or not. He wouldn't be the one to turn on her. She had been heaven sent for him and he would be loyal to her until death. That afternoon, Barney sought Iris privately.

"Missus Blackheart, that soldier's been asking lots of questions about you all day."

Iris looked frustrated. "He did that to me last night too. I wonder what he's up to ... Just keep an eye on him for me, Barney. Maybe it's nothing."

"Ma'am, is there anything I'm not supposed to tell him? I didn't give him big answers today. I promise not to get you into trouble. Are you in trouble?" Barney wanted to know.

Iris shook her head to assure him. "No. Don't fear. There's nothing you could say that would do harm." Iris hoped that Hattie had not told him everything about their past. But even if she had, it was nothing that would jeopardize her with the Union soldier.

By the end of the week, David had asked everyone in town all they knew about Missus Blackheart. Always, he was told the same answer. She was from Georgia, come up for her health, husband died, bought the house, freed her slave, went to church, had many friends and was well respected. The answers added up, but there was something in her eyes when he questioned her. David could see fear. He knew she was hiding something and it was his job to find out what it was.

On Saturday morning, Iris and Hattie left with the children to have tea with the elderly Missus Reed. They had grown a lovely friendship over the last three years and Iris looked forward to tea twice a month with her friend. Barney stayed behind to begin work on his new home. The Lieutenant was to help. After thirty minutes sawing down nearby trees, David put his plan into action. He pretended to grow dizzy and grabbed his head.

"My head's spinning, Barney," he spoke as if in pain. "I must be getting sick. I'm going back to the house to lie down for a while. I'll be back as soon as this goes away."

"Sure, Mister Stoneman. Need anything?" Barney asked, believing the man.

"No. I'll be all right. Just … need to rest."

David walked slowly toward the house and went inside. He immediately went upstairs to Missus Blackheart's room. He pulled out bureau drawers, feeling inside for papers of any kind. He rifled through her under-drawers and camisoles, stockings and shifts. He made his way over to a cabinet full of dresses and searched through those. He found money and jewelry in a box, but no incriminating evidence. Maybe she was telling the truth after all. He decided to look over near the bed. There was a Bible on a small table. Inside was one of the Confederate casualty lists from South Carolina. Over four dozen names were marked. David caught his breath. This was something! If she were truly from Georgia, why did she have a list from another state? And was this a real list, or some spy information? Something was definitely not right. David continued searching the room for more clues, but found nothing. Knowing Missus Blackheart would return within the hour, David retreated to the parlor to wait. She had some explaining to do.

The walk home had been stressful to say the least. Little Ruthy had cried the entire time. Noah had whined and whimpered, desperately needing a nap. Iris and Hattie were much relieved to see the house at last, anxious to put the children to bed. When they entered the parlor though, Iris immediately noticed the look on the lieutenant's face. Hattie walked off with her children.

"You look as sour as I feel," Iris told him.

The soldier stood at his chair. "Why don't you take a seat, Missus Blackheart."

"Is something the matter?" she asked wearily. "I'd really like to go upstairs ..."

"Depends," he interrupted, holding up the sheet of paper from South Carolina. "Can you explain this to me, Madam?"

Iris took the paper as her heart pounded. Once she saw what it was, her eyes came up slowly. Her expression was stunned.

"Tell me Missus Blackheart, if that's really your name, what a Georgia woman is doing with a big list of casualties from South Carolina?" he demanded loudly. "In fact, I doubt this is a real list. I think it's spy information. You've been lying to me! You aren't from Georgia at all! What are you doing here? I want to know! It's my job to find out. Are you a spy?" he nearly shouted as he stepped closer to where she stood.

Iris tried to back up, but the door was in the way. Fear, anger, hurt and dismay filled her soul. She looked the lieutenant in the face, completely speechless. However, all the courage she had shot into her right hand and she slapped him soundly across the cheek.

"How dare you!" she seethed in a most unlady-like manner. "This is private! You pig! You dog!" she shouted back at him. She side-stepped to go around him, but the lieutenant caught her by the arm.

"I know you have a secret. I'm going to find out what it is, Madam," he breathed out.

"Let go of me," she demanded, jerking on her arm. "Barney, help!" she screamed.

The lieutenant covered her mouth with his hand and pushed her body up against the wall to hold her in place. "Be quiet, woman. You've lied to a Union officer. That's an offense that could get you jailed. How would you like that? Ever seen the inside of a prison? It's not very nice. I want the truth from you, or I'll take you away," he warned. The man pulled Iris away from the wall and pushed her down to sit on the couch. He stood above her with his hands on his hips. "Move and you'll regret it. Now, I want to know, are you from Georgia or not?"

Iris began to cry. Hattie emerged from the back room with a broom in hand, ready to defend her mistress. David ordered her to return or risk being arrested for interfering. Hattie looked at Iris for instructions. Iris nodded.

"Go back to your children, Hattie," she sniffled.

Not at all happy, Hattie retreated. Her face showed both fear and concern.

David returned his gaze to the woman on the couch. How unfortunate that she was so beautiful. It would be a great waste of womanhood when she was hanged for spying. She was still crying. David stomped his boot on the ground. "Now, woman! Answer me! Are you from Georgia?"

With her spirit finally broken, Iris shook her head.

David grinned with satisfaction. He knew it! "What is this?" he demanded, thrusting the so-called casualty list in her face.

"A casualty list."

"Ha!" he laughed. "You expect me to believe that?"

Iris looked up at him with water-filled eyes. "That's what it is. It's where I'm from."

"If you're from South Carolina, what town did you live in? And don't say Gordon, there's no such place," he warned.

Iris shook her head. "Lexington."

He raised an eyebrow in disbelief. "What are you doing here?"

"Nothing," she told him truthfully. "Just … living."

"Don't lie, woman! I'm not buying your story. Why are all these names circled? What are you really up to?"

"Honestly? Nothing," Iris sobbed. "I knew those people on that list. That's all. I just used to know them when I was younger."

David still did not believe her. "Where's your husband then, because I don't think you're really a widow."

Iris was quiet for a moment, then she shrugged her shoulders. "I don't know where he is."

David was furious. All these lies! She was definitely the person he'd been looking for. He snatched the woman up by the arm and shouted in her face, "What's your real name, woman?"

Terrified, Iris wailed. "Iris Elaine Picket," she shouted. Her heart was pounding and she felt faint.

"Missus Picket, I'll ask again, where is your husband?"

Iris shook her head. "I don't know, I don't know, I don't know."

"Why are you really here?" David demanded again.

Iris wiped her eyes with the palms of her hands. Her safe make-believe world was crashing down. "I ran away," she sobbed. "He beat me. I ran away before the war started. He would have killed me."

David stopped short. What? Was this truth? The woman looked terrified. He loosened his grip on her arm. "Got any proof?" he asked in a normal tone of voice.

Iris nodded as she slumped onto the floor. Her bottom lip quivered. "I have a letter. It's for my mother, in case, anything happens to me," she spoke in broken sobs.

"Get it."

After a few deep breaths, Iris reached into the front of her dress. She adjusted the corset enough to pull out a worn envelope. This she handed to the lieutenant before casting her eyes to the floor. She was tempted to lie down in utter exhaustion.

David took the worn letter and opened the envelope. Inside, he read instructions on what to do in case Missus Picket's body was deceased. It gave the address of her mother in Charleston and the reason for her current situation. David couldn't believe it. The letter sure seemed genuine. Either that or she was the best spy and liar he'd ever known. Could he have been wrong about her? He had his first doubts. David tucked the letter into his vest. "I'll just keep this for a little while," he spoke calmly. "To verify your story."

Iris made no move to acknowledge his words.

"Madam, I apologize. I might have made a grave error upon you," David offered. "I will be leaving today and will not bother you again. Unless of course, your story proves to be false. In the future, it would be wise not to inquire about enemy information. We are at war, you know. It looks suspicious and you may not be so lucky to get off next time." With that, Lieutenant Stoneman turned to go upstairs. He would pack his bag and leave for there was no more work to be done here.

While in his rented room, David heard another door close nearby. He assumed Missus Picket had gone to her room. He left payment for the week on his dresser and walked into the hallway. David left the boarding house, feeling like a heel for treating this woman so badly.

Nothing more came of that event. Barney had not heard her cries for he'd been too far away. And the lieutenant had told no one, for not one town member mentioned anything of it. Iris continued to live as Missus Blackheart. The war raged on through fall and winter. Iris caught bits of news from guests who came through the boardinghouse, and occasionally she read newspapers from major cities in the north. She learned of Sherman's march through Georgia and wondered how South Carolina was holding up. She wanted word of her parents' safety, but knew it was too risky to find out. All she could do was pray.

On April first, eighteen sixty-five, Iris received a letter. There was no return address on the envelope. She opened it carefully, wondering who would have sent her a letter. Inside was a recent killed-in-action list from South Carolina. Iris looked down at two names that had been circled: Bently James Picket, and Johnathan Wayne Picket. Iris' legs gave way and she collapsed onto the floor. Emotions overwhelmed her body. She began to shake and cry. He was dead. Johnathan was dead. She was safe. She was free.

Hattie heard her mistress crying. She put down the bowl in her hands and walked to the parlor. "What is it?" she asked fearfully. Hattie bent over as best she could in her condition to coax her mistress off the floor.

"He's dead, Hattie. He's gone. Dead," Iris told her.

"Who, ma'am?" Hattie wondered.

"Johnathan. He's gone. Killed in the war. I'm finally free, Hattie," she whispered, still shaking.

Hattie nodded. "I'm glad, ma'am." Hattie watched as Iris came to terms with her new position. She really was a widow now. And free from fear. Hattie grabbed the papers. "Who sent this?"

Iris' breath came in small gasps. "I ... don't know." But when she reached for the envelope again, another letter fell out. It was her letter, the one Lieutenant Stoneman had taken seven months ago. In small script along the bottom, he had written these words:

My deepest apologies. LDS.

Her mouth dropped open. "It's from that horrid lieutenant!" she spoke loudly. Iris wanted to throw the papers on the ground simply because that man had touched them. "Why would he send this to me? It's been months since he was here. Doesn't he know I never want to think about him again?" she growled. She looked at the list again to find the date. It was only a month old. She shook her head. "Of all the gall ... Over half a year? I can't believe he remembered!" This time she did throw all the papers on the floor in disgust.

Hattie watched curiously. "Maybe he felt bad for how he treated you," she offered.

"Well ... he should," Iris spoke in anger.

"Does this mean you'll be goin' back when the war's over?" Hattie asked next.

Iris sighed heavily. "I don't know, Hattie. I just don't know."

8

April 9, 1865

General Lee of the Confederacy surrendered to General Grant of the Union at the Appomatox Courthouse. Within days, the news spread all over the country. Men were released from prison to begin the long journey home. Slaves from the south left their masters to begin a new free life. Husbands were reunited with their wives and children. Women wept for sons and husbands lost in the war. Everyone clung to the hope that life would be normal again. Southerners, however, had to begin a new way of living without their slaves. Along with Reconstruction, it was a difficult plight. Carpetbaggers descended from the north to take advantage of business and political situations. To make matters worse, President Lincoln was shot dead on Good Friday. An already wounded nation mourned.

Iris decided by the end of April that it was safe enough to write a letter to her mother. She told her mother where she was and caught her up on the last four years. Iris told her mother that she knew Johnathan was dead. She also told her that Hattie had married and now had two children.

Mother, I miss you dearly. Always loving you and Tom, Iris.

Iris was walking to the train station to deliver the letter when she ran into the elderly Missus Reed. "How are you today," she asked.

The white-haired woman smiled with a nod. "Missus Black-heart, hello. I am good, very good. I just received a letter from my grandson. He's alive! He's coming up to see me next month. He was captured as a prisoner and spent eleven months in prison. He says I won't recognize him."

Iris remembered the young man who had helped her so kindly that night of the party. She was glad that he had survived. "I'm glad he's coming to see you," Iris smiled.

The woman's eyes twinkled. "Say, Missus Blackheart, when Samuel arrives, I will have to introduce the two of you. You must be about the same age. Let's see now, Sam would be …" she paused for thought. "About twenty-six now."

"I'm sure he's very nice, Missus Reed, but I'm not looking for another husband. Thanks all the same though," she spoke politely.

"Why not, deary?" the woman pressed. "You are still young. And pretty too. There's still a chance for children. A man would be good for you."

That was the last thing she wanted. Iris did not want to hurt Missus Reed's feelings, but she did want her to stop meddling into her private business. At last, Iris decided to be frank. "Missus Reed, may I tell you something?"

The elderly woman nodded. "Of course, dear."

For some reason, Iris felt her pulse increase. "My first husband beat me. He beat me and killed our unborn child. I don't like the thought of having another husband, ma'am, because my first one was so terrible. Do you understand?"

The grandmother looked horrified, but then she came over and gave Iris a hug. "I'm sorry, dear. You must know that not all men are like that. My James was wonderful and good as gold to me. You must have faith that God will not let you down. Pray for a good husband, and He will send you one in time if it's His will."

Iris accepted the woman's advice as one would take it from a child. Both women continued on their way after that. Iris mailed her letter and enjoyed the springtime afternoon stroll as she headed home. There was still a little coolness in the air, but today was definitely the warmest day so far this year. As she neared her house, Iris noticed a man rocking on her front porch. He wore a gentleman's clothes. She assumed he wanted to rent a room for the night. As she came closer however, his face became unquestioningly familiar. It was Lieutenant Stoneman!

Iris swallowed the lump in her throat and fought the urge to grab a fistful of soil. She did clench her fists defensively though, ready for a fight.

Lieutenant David Stoneman was haunted by thoughts of this pretty woman he had so terribly wronged. He had spent the entire remainder of the war thinking how he could ask her forgiveness and become her friend. He wanted to give her comfort in any way possible. In fact, he was willing to marry her, to give her a wonderful second marriage. She had showed real spirit and character. He liked that. Besides, he really did want a wife. He was twenty-eight and these last four years had been terribly long. He knew now what he wanted. Her name was Iris.

As she entered the yard, David stood and removed his hat. "Ma'am," he spoke gently.

Iris decided that the best course of action would be to ignore him. She made a beeline for the front door.

He fiddled with his hat. "I guess you're wondering what I'm doing here," he stated awkwardly.

She couldn't do it. Iris snapped and turned on him with narrowed eyes. "No, actually. I don't give you much thought at all."

"Fair enough," he agreed. "Did you get my letter?"

Iris clenched her teeth, and nodded.

"Was one of those men your husband?" he asked bluntly.

"Yes."

"So you can go home now, if you want," he hinted. "Are you going home?"

"I don't see how that's any of your business, Lieutenant," she shot back rudely.

David cleared his throat. "You see, I was hoping to rent a room from you for a few days."

Was he insane? "Why are you here?" she demanded.

"To ask your forgiveness," he answered honestly. "And to explain why I treated you so badly."

Iris wasn't sure she wanted to hear his story, and she certainly was not ready to forgive him for rough handling her the way he had. But in the last week, she'd only had one other boarder, and her coffers were getting low.

"If I let you stay here, your rent is triple the normal rate," she blurted. Money was money after all, and she was a business woman. She didn't have to like him.

David smiled. "Agreed."

"Supper's at six." That's all she said before going into the house and up to her room. Iris needed a moment to regain her composure. Hattie needed her downstairs to help with the meal, but she was just going to have to wait a few minutes.

Just before supper, a family of four arrived to stay the night on their way south. The two children, a twelve-year-old boy and a ten-year-old girl, took one room. Their parents took the other. Much to Iris' relief, the dinner table was full. She had no desire at all to share Mister Stoneman's company. David and the man, a Mister Morgan, spent the evening discussing the war and the future of the country. Iris was glad to have the company of Missus Morgan and her two children. They were headed to Philadelphia to visit relatives.

Later in the evening, the two women took up sewing in the parlor. The men went outside for a walk to further discuss politics. When they returned an hour later, David handed Iris a bunch of wild flowers that he'd picked.

"For your hospitality, ma'am," he told her in front of the Morgan family.

Not wanting to make a scene, Iris accepted them, excusing herself to put the flowers in water. Upon returning to the room, she shot David a warning glance. She wanted no funny business from him. Around nine o'clock, the children were told to go to bed. Missus Morgan walked over to her hostess and whispered. "I saw that you offer hot baths. I'd like one, please."

Iris nodded. She had turned Hattie's old room into a private wash room, complete with tub.

"I'll find Barney to get it set up for you, mam. If you all will excuse me," she told the guests. David was speaking with Mister Morgan, but stood politely when she left the room.

Barney answered and looked quite sleepy.

"Sorry Barney, but I need your help to get a bath ready for Missus Morgan. I'll put the water on the stove, but can you come in fifteen minutes to carry it for me?"

He nodded and shut the door.

When Iris returned to the kitchen, David was waiting for her. "May I help you?" he offered.

"No thank you," she replied, giving him the cold shoulder. "I can manage it fine." Iris grabbed the rope handles of the four buckets sitting on the floor.

"May I walk with you then?"

Iris shook her head. "Lieutenant, I don't want your company. Do you understand?"

"Yes. I understand. But my conscience insists that I speak with you," he professed.

"Once you speak it, will you leave me alone?" she asked.

He nodded.

"Very well. Tell me while I draw water."

Outside, as they headed to the well, David began speaking. "You see Missus Picket, I just wanted to let you know how very sorry I am for the way I treated you last fall. I want you to know, under normal circumstances, that I am a gentleman. I was brought up to treat a lady with respect." He stopped for a moment. Iris said nothing, so he continued. "I am from a good family in Hartford, Connecticut. When I came here to investigate you, I was searching for a Confederate spy. It was rumored it was a woman. My best friend had just been killed a month earlier because a spy had leaked important information. It sabotaged his mission. Angry, I made it my mission to find the spy who'd done this. I thought it was you. I beg your forgiveness, Madam."

David grabbed the two full buckets of water while Iris took the third and fourth. He followed her back into the house. Silently, Iris poured the water into pots on the stove. She considered his confession. Maybe, maybe she could understand his behavior. If her friend had been killed, she might have done the same thing, if she were a man. Iris frowned. Deep down, she knew what she had to do. At the time, David had only acted according to the Union Army's best information during a time of war. Mistakes happened.

"Did you find the real spy?" she finally asked.

"Yes."

"Was it a woman?"

"No. But it was a man masquerading as a woman," he explained.

"What happened to him?"

David frowned, afraid to speak the truth.

"You hung him?" she asked.

He nodded.

"I will forgive you Lieutenant," she answered stoically. Iris knew it was the Christian thing to do.

Immediately, David sighed. "Thank you. Thank you."

Iris watched as this man humbled himself before her. It was strange. She had never seen a man begging forgiveness from a woman before. After his second 'thank you,' she held up her hand. "Very well. Now, please excuse me while I see to this bath water."

David Stoneman excused himself for the evening and retired to his room. He was so happy inside that he had been forgiven. It was like a huge weight had been lifted from his shoulders. It was a marvelous thing, to know he was now in her good will. David slept well that night.

Iris, however, was completely disturbed by his admissions. How strange this man was to care so much about how she felt toward him. Especially considering they had only known each other for a matter of days during the war. What would her opinion matter to a soldier like him? She was just a woman of no significance in his life. Iris rolled over in bed trying to sort out her thoughts. Suddenly, a new idea entered her mind. Oh no. What if she was more to him than a passing acquaintance? Oh no! She would have to set him straight first thing in the morning. But what about other men? The war was over. Men would be returning home. Some would want wives. Iris shook her head. Men were nothing but trouble.

Iris slept poorly, waking just at dawn with dark rings under her eyes. She struggled to get out of bed. It had become her habit, now that Hattie had children, to get up and help make breakfast for all the guests. Iris forced herself out of bed and dressed in a simple cotton garment the color of a mauve sky. She braided her long black hair and pinned it into a spiral on her head.

Downstairs, Iris pulled on a striped apron and started a pot of strong coffee. It was unusual for Hattie not to be already in the kitchen. Iris wondered where she was. She pulled out some oats to boil and some bacon to fry. Finally, Barney arrived with a bucket of fresh milk from their only cow.

"Where is Mary Grace this morning?" Iris asked.

"Ma'am, she ain't feeling too good today. Her stomach's all hurting inside. She asked to stay in bed today. I'm here to help though," he answered.

"Don't worry, Barney, I've got it. You go mind your wife and children," Iris told him. Oh but it hurt to say it. She was already so, so tired.

"Thank you, ma'am. You sure?"

Iris nodded. Inside, her heart was low. Why today, of all days, was Hattie not available? Setting her mind to get all the work done alone, Iris continued her preparations.

The Morgan children were the first to arrive in the kitchen.

"That smells good, ma'am," the boy said, eager to eat.

"May I help you, ma'am?' the girl asked.

"Yes. That would be wonderful," Iris answered. "You can find the brown sugar and raisins in the cupboard for the oatmeal. Paul, if you could set the table for me, please. The dishes are in that cabinet."

"But that's woman's work!" the boy exclaimed.

David entered the room at that time and heard the boy's comment. "Young man, your hostess has asked you to do something. Have some respect for your elders and do it," he told him.

The boy's face fell. "Yes, sir."

Iris looked at David and offered him a small smile of appreciation. David was pleased. It was the first smile she had offered him.

"Can I help too?" he asked.

"If you want to. The children need milk poured. I have coffee for you if you want some."

The four of them set out to finish the work and completed their tasks just as the Morgan parents came down the stairwell.

"Good morning," they greeted with bright smiles.

After breakfast, Mister Morgan paid their hostess for the rooms. "We had a great night of sleep, thanks so much. We'll stop back by on our way home at the end of summer," he told her.

"Until then," Iris answered. She waved as the wagon pulled away.

Once they were gone, Iris decided to check on Hattie. David watched her from the porch. She knocked on the Montgomery's door. Barney opened it and let her inside. When Iris came back, she had both children in tow. She had offered to watch them for the day so Hattie could have some quiet while she rested. Her face had been drawn in pain as her large swollen belly cramped. Iris knew it was too early for the baby to come. Hattie had at least six more weeks to go. Iris said a little prayer for her friend and the unborn child. Barney would keep vigil over his wife for the day.

"Children, what shall we do?" Iris asked them.

"Go see Mis'er Brown puppies!" Noah said excitedly.

"All right. We can go see the puppies," she told them. "Let me go get my hat and we will walk over there."

Iris left Noah in the yard to play for a moment while she went quickly inside to fetch her straw hat. Ten-month-old Ruthy was content to be held. The sun was warm and shining brightly today, so it was a good day to be outside.

David Stoneman was still on the porch watching Noah when Iris came out of the house. "May I come too?" he asked. "I've nothing to do today."

Iris lifted a shoulder like she didn't care. "Suit yourself," she replied nonchalantly.

The foursome then headed down the road and across the field to the Brown farm.

"I grew up in the city most of my life until the war," David told her after a while. "I was working with my father in the bank. He was wounded at Gettysburg, had his right arm amputated. It grieved him terribly, but my mother is glad he is still alive. We lost two of my brothers though."

Iris was silent for a moment while she thought about his words. "Sorry about your brothers. I know nothing of my family yet. I just sent a letter to my mother yesterday."

"Do you have any brothers or sisters?" he asked.

"No."

David continued the conversation. "I have two sisters. They both still live with my folks. Their beaus were killed."

"That's ... very sad."

"Hurry, puppy, please!" the little boy called out. He was so anxious to get to the farm and the grown-ups were taking forever.

"I can go ahead with him if you want me to," David offered.

Iris had a very slow Ruthy by the hands, helping the young person learn to walk. "If you like."

She watched as David scooped Noah into his arms and carried him on his high shoulders. Noah squealed with delight when David began to run. "Show me the way," he called out to his little passenger. Noah pointed toward the far end of the field.

Iris snickered as she continued to walk slowly with the little girl. Ruthy was taking in her surroundings, looking at every flower, every blade of grass, investigating every rock along the way. It was nearly twenty minutes later when they arrived at the Brown farm.

She found David, Noah and Mister Brown in the yard with the litter of brown furry puppies.

Noah giggled as the little creatures rolled around him. He sat on the ground, legs folded with one in his lap while others tried to climb up. David and Mister Brown were engaged in a friendly conversation.

"Good day, Missus Blackheart," the farmer greeted when he spotted her.

"Hello, Mister Brown. It's a nice day," she answered. Iris watched as Noah tried to pick up a puppy with both hands around its neck."

"Oh no baby, not like that. Here, let me show you," she told the little boy. Iris ran over to save the poor puppy. Both men chuckled as Iris showed Noah how to scoop the animal into his arms. "Do not hold it around the neck, Noah. It will die if you do," she explained gently.

Noah held onto the squirming animal as it tried to climb up his neck. It licked him on the neck and lips. Noah squealed again.

"Looks like he's making new friends," Mister Brown stated.

"Yes, it does," David agreed. "When will those pups be weaned?"

"In about another week," the good farmer replied.

Iris did not hear their conversation, for she was playing with the puppies herself. They were wonderfully adorable. Maybe she would get one for the children when the time came. Hattie would be busy soon with the new baby, and the children would need some entertainment.

After an hour at the farm, Ruthy began to get fussy. It was time for her morning nap. "I'd better be getting along with this one," Iris told the men. "David, you'll bring Noah home when he's ready?" she asked.

David looked up and nodded. "Yes. We might stop in town first though. There's something I need to order."

"Very well. See that Noah's home by noon, because he gets a nap after eating," she reminded him.

Grinning, David replied, "Yes, ma'am."

One month later, at the end of May, Hattie was still in bed. Her pregnancy was not going well and she had swollen up quite large. The doctor had been called from town and he told her just to rest until the baby came. That was all he could do for her right now. He also warned Barney not to make any more children. Further pregnancies would do more harm than good.

With Hattie on bedrest, Iris was doing all of the housework, as well as the cooking. David helped out too by entertaining the children. He had stayed on during the month to help and was working on a secret project with Noah. They giggled about it every night at supper.

"What are you two snickering about? Iris teased them one night.

Noah looked at her with a wide grin. "It's a seeecret!" he said in a silly voice.

David grinned with a wink. Over the last month, Iris had come to terms with this lieutenant. He was nice, and she did genuinely forgive him for the past. He had shown himself to be a gentleman and a good Christian. He prayed at every meal, spent time in his Bible every night, and took them all to church on Sunday. They were fast becoming good friends.

"Run and get the doctor!" Barney shouted from the front door. "I've got to stay with Mary Grace." He ran back to their cabin as fast as he could go. Iris heard her good friend scream in pain. David leapt up from the table and bound out the door in a dead sprint.

"Children, you stay here and finish your supper," Iris told them. She then quickly hurried over to find out what was happening.

Hattie's dark face was ashen. Her eyes were closed against the pain. "What's happening?" Iris asked, fearful for her friend's life.

"It ain't right," Barney told her fearfully. "Not like the others. And it's too soon. Much too soon."

"Oh, please God!" Hattie cried out between short breaths.

Iris was scared. She hoped David would return soon with the doctor. "I'll get water and some towels," she told Barney. She ran back to her own home and told the children, "Your momma is going to have another baby soon." She tried to sound cheerful. "How would you like to sleep upstairs in the big house tonight?"

Noah was eager to sleep in one of the big fancy beds. "Yes, ma'am!" he exclaimed. Eleven-month-old Ruth just smiled and blinked.

Iris started a pot of water to purify and ran upstairs to get some clean sheets. She also put the children to bed. Quickly as she could, she returned to Hattie.

"She passed out," Barney explained in a shaky voice. He felt so helpless. "I guess that's best for now. She's still breathing," he added, scared to death for the life of his wonderful wife.

Iris could see tears filling up in Barney's eyes. How wonderful to have a man care so deeply for his wife. Barney was a better husband to Hattie than Johnathan had been to her. There was no doubt. Iris searched her mind for something to say to him. "Maybe you could go out and watch for the doctor," she suggested.

"No, ma'am. I won't leave her side," he insisted loyally.

Iris choked back the lump in her throat. "Very well, Barney. You're such a good man."

Half an hour later, the doctor arrived with a new assistant. David was brought back as well on the back of the doctor's buggy. He was sorely exhausted from running to find the doctor. He headed for the porch to catch his breath.

"Ma'am," Doctor White greeted. "This is Doctor McCory. He's serving under me."

"Ma'am," the younger doctor greeted with a handshake.

The doctors entered the cabin and greeted Barney. "Mister Montgomery, we'll do the best we can for her," he assured the nervous husband. "Would you mind stepping outside?"

"I won't leave her, Doctor," Barney stated with his quivering voice.

Doctor White was gentle with him. "Barney, this may not be very pretty. Please, will you have faith in me?"

Barney wasn't happy, but he nodded.

"Has her water broken?" the new physician asked.

"No, not yet," Iris supplied. She knew this much at least.

"They've not been regular pains, Doctor," Barney added. "Not like with the other two."

"Very well. If you will both step outside please," Doctor White requested.

Iris touched Barney on the shoulder. They should do what the doctor's asked. Outside, Iris leaned against the cabin wall. Barney started pacing nervously. After only a minute, Doctor McCory opened the door.

"Mister Montgomery, we need to operate on your wife."

Barney let out a wail of grief.

"There were two babies. One is lodged and the other cannot get out. Please remain outside. This should take no more than an hour." Without waiting longer, he shut the door.

Barney collapsed onto the ground sobbing. He sat there with his head buried in his hands. Surely God would not take her away from him. Surely not after all he'd suffered in his life. Wasn't he deserving of a little happiness? How could he be happy if his beloved soul mate was gone?

Iris went rather numb. David came over from the porch to ask what was happening. She explained what she knew. His face looked grim.

"Come, Barney. Let's take a short walk."

They only made it as far as the barn. Barney sat down on a stump that was waiting to be chopped into firewood. He was simply too weak to stand. Iris sat on her own front steps. This hour would be one of the longest in her life. She used the time to pray earnestly for Hattie and the children.

It was dark outside now. The evening was filled with far off calls of birds and insects. Stars twinkled overhead in the infinite sky. How peaceful and pleasant the world seemed from this view

– like nothing bad had ever happened in the world. Iris breathed in the comfortable mountain air. It filled her soul with a sense of tranquility.

At last, the new physician emerged from the cabin with a small bundle in his arms. Everyone looked up from the porch. The dim lights from the two houses barely lit the yard. Barney stood up, waiting like a man for the bad news.

Doctor McCory smiled at the group of people. "Your son, Mister Montgomery," he spoke softy.

"Glory!" Barney whispered in awe. "My wife?"

"She will recover, in time. It will take a month for her to mend." He paused. "Only one child survived. I am sorry. The other was a boy as well."

Barney nodded and took his living son. He was crying grateful tears now; they were streaming down his dark skin. "Can I see Mary Grace?" he blubbered. The little face wrapped in the bundle was perfect and round. Dark eyes stared at the sky above in wonder.

"Yes, but she's still out from the either," he doctor explained.

Barney held tightly to his new little boy as he headed inside. In his heart, he thanked God for all his blessings, great and small.

In the yard, Iris turned to the physician. "Can I make you some coffee?"

Doctor McCory turned to the pretty widow. "Yes, please." Doctor White had told him a little about her story. He was glad she was no longer in mourning and off limits. Her pretty calico dress confirmed that status. He would have to call upon her soon.

A few days later, on a drizzling Sunday, David and Iris walked to church. Iris' parasol shielded her from the rain. It had been a bittersweet week. The Montgomery family had buried the stillborn boy in a small grave beside their house. Hattie had been too weak to grieve properly, but she knew there had been two boys. She was, however, happy to have one that was alive and well. He was tiny, albeit, because of his early birth, but still healthy. Noah was not so thrilled about the baby. It took his father's attentions and made his momma sick. And to make matters worse, he had to be quiet all the time. That was no fun at all.

Hattie was still in much pain. Iris had worked tirelessly to care for the house, the children, and nurse her friend. Iris needed the comforting solace of church.

"Maybe all this rain will bring meadows full of summer flowers," David spoke as they walked.

Iris thought about his statement deeply. He spoke as though he might actually be around to see them. "Lieutenant, may I ask you a question," she queried.

"Certainly."

"I was wondering, when do you report back to duty? I mean, how long do you plan to stay in Williamsport?"

He smiled a crooked grin. "I was wondering when you would get suspicious. I do plan to return home, eventually, unless I find something else."

"Something else?" she asked. "Explain."

David took a long breath. Should he be honest at this point? He wasn't sure she was ready yet. "I have something in mind, but the timing isn't right yet," he allowed without details. How could he possibly tell her he wanted a wife? He wanted her.

"Well, I wish you luck then," she answered with sincerity. She had grown to respect David as a friend. He had been invaluable help these last few weeks.

When they entered the church, David asked in a hushed voice, "Will it embarrass you if I sit by you again?"

Iris smirked and shook her head. David was reassured by this. Maybe in time, she might actually learn to love him. He hoped.

Once they were seated, the new doctor walked over. "How's Missus Montgomery? I plan to stop by this week to check on her."

"She's in a lot of pain," Iris replied, not noticing how he looked at her.

David saw it. He saw the look of admiration in the young man's eyes. How he took her entire body into his glance. David saw it, because he did the same thing when he was close to her. This was going to be trouble.

"She probably will be, for a while. I could give her something, but she would pass it to the baby when she nursed. It wouldn't be safe," he offered confidently. Doctor McCory then turned to David. "I hear you are fresh off the field, Lieutenant Stoneman. Who'd you serve under?"

"General McClellan," David answered shortly.

The doctor nodded. "Fine. You seem to have come out without a scratch. Most of my friends weren't so lucky."

David nodded. "Mine neither."

"Allen McCory, sir. Served in the field myself. Learned my trade fresh on the battle field. I could sure tell you some stories," he rambled. "You headed home now?"

"Not quite," David replied. He wished he could shoo this man away like a pesky fly.

The preacher stepped up to the front of the church and took his place in the pulpit. Allen excused himself and returned to his seat next to Doctor White. Iris noticed that all of the young women in the church kept looking at both the new doctor and the lieutenant sitting beside her. Once, she stole a glance around and the new doctor was smiling at her. Quickly, she had to look away.

At the end of the service, the preacher told everyone he had a special announcement. "Since the war is over, we have much to celebrate. The return of our men and boys who made it through and the promise of new life with spring. It is my honor to announce that we will resume our annual June dance in two weeks," he told them all.

Everyone who was familiar with the town's traditions clapped their approval. The women smiled, and the older girls giggled with delight. The young men nodded eagerly as well, anxious to match up with the females. Iris guessed there were about eighty-five people in the church. It would make for a fun celebration. She had not been to a party since Hattie's wedding three years ago.

"That will be fun," David said to her as they left.

Iris was nodding just as they were about to walk out the door. Missus Reed caught Iris by the arm. "Missus Blackheart," she called out strongly. "I want to introduce you to my grandson, Samuel."

9

First week of June, 1865

I ris' eyes grew wide when she saw Samuel. The war had aged him considerably. He wore a full beard and walked with a cane.

"Samuel, this is Missus Blackheart," the senior woman spoke. Sam's eyes showed confusion. He knew this woman. She was familiar.

"Hello, Ma'am. Sam Reed," he offered, extending his hand.

"How do you do?" Iris responded, wondering if he recognized her. There really was no reason to hide her true identity any more. She was safe now.

"Have you ever been to Lexington, South Carolina, ma'am?" he asked. "You look so familiar, but I can't place you."

Iris' heart was working faster. She felt the thumping in her chest. "Yes," she answered honestly. "I have, Mister Reed. And you have met me before. You rescued me one night at a party when I wasn't feeling well. You were kind enough to take me home."

Samuel's eyes grew wide. "Missus Picket?" he questioned with astonishment.

"Yes. It's me."

Missus Reed looked confused and surprised.

"Did you remarry?" her grandson questioned. The group had stepped aside so others could leave the church. They were all nearly alone now. Sam glanced at David.

"You know each other?" Missus Reed asked in two octaves.

"Yes, ma'am," Sam replied. "We met once, just before the war."

"But, why did you call her Missus Picket? I told you dear, her name is Blackheart," the elderly woman repeated.

Iris looked down at the floor, slightly ashamed for lying to this Godly woman. "Actually, ma'am, my name is Missus Picket."

Missus Reed brought a hand up to her temple. "Samuel, what is going on? Why don't I understand?"

"Ma'am, why don't you and Samuel come over to the house for dinner? I can explain everything," Iris offered.

The grandmother nodded.

David cleared his throat. Iris had forgotten he was standing beside her. "Oh, Mister Reed, this is Lieutenant Stoneman."

The men shook hands politely. Iris took Missus Reed by the hand and walked outside. "You see, ma'am, remember when I told you that I had a husband who beat me? I ran away from him. I escaped to come here before the war started. I changed my name so he wouldn't be able to find me and I came all the way up here to hide and start a new life. I've been living as Missus Blackheart, but my real name is Iris Elaine Picket. I was not a widow when I came here, but I am now. Lieutenant Stoneman helped me find that out. I am safe now, for the first time in over five years."

Missus Reed was stunned. "Oh my dear!" was all she could manage.

"I haven't heard from my mother in four years. I don't know if she or my stepfather are alive or dead. I did send them a letter, but I haven't heard back from them yet. I don't know for certain that I should return. Johnathan's spies might still have it out for me. Who knows what they'd do ..." Iris thought darkly.

The grandmother turned to her grandson. "Did you know all this, Sam?" she asked.

Samuel shook his head. "No, ma'am. All I knew was that she was a sad woman."

It had stopped raining for the moment. Iris was glad the truth was finally getting out. It would be nice to be called by her real first name again. She would tell Hattie they could both stop pretending now. Then Iris turned to Sam.

"Do you have any news of my stepfather? Tom Payton is his name, from Charleston."

He shook his head. "Sorry. I'm afraid I do not."

Iris continued. "Did you know that my husband was dead?"

He nodded this time. "Yes, ma'am. That I did know. He was killed by Sherman's troops as they came through South Carolina."

Iris felt a little satisfaction in hearing it. "I would like to speak with you during supper, if you don't mind," she told Sam. "About the people from back home. I want to know what has happened. Have you been back to Lexington?"

"No. I haven't. My father was killed several years ago, and our land destroyed. I have nothing to return to there. But I did have Grandmother here, at least, I hoped she was still here. So when I was released from prison, I immediately headed north," he explained sadly.

"What happened to your leg?" David asked.

"Caught a bullet just below the knee. I was lucky though. Kept my leg and kept my life," Sam answered humbly.

"I'm wondering, how you two can be speaking to one another," the grandmother stated frankly. "A Johnny Reb and a true blue Yank."

"Hatred comes from politics, ma'am, not people," David spoke quickly with sincerity.

She made a noise in her throat in surprise. "Very good, young man."

The group finally reached Iris' home. The Montgomery children were playing in the yard with their father. The two women went inside to prepare food. The men remained on the porch, chatting lightly about the warm weather, the upcoming dance and other easy topics. They both purposely avoided discussing war and politics. After a short while, Mister Brown came walking down the road carrying two soft brown pups.

"They're here," David said to Noah.

"Are the little houses for the pups, Miss'r Stoneman?" Noah asked of their shared secret project.

"Yes, they are," David affirmed.

Noah looked frustrated. "I's hoping mama's new baby could live there too," he stated honestly.

"No," David chuckled. "The houses are not for the baby."

Mister Brown heard some of the conversation and grinned. He set down the two playful puppies. Ruth screamed and crawled after them.

"Thanks, Miss'r Brown," Noah told the farmer.

David smiled at the children. He knew this week had been tough on them. These little dogs were going to bring them some joy.

"What's all the commotion?" Iris asked from the doorway. She saw the two children following the puppies around the yard. She shot a glance at David.

He saw her and smiled. "Look what the children just got," he offered innocently.

"Puppies?" she asked.

David nodded. Iris looked at Samuel who still sat in a chair. He was smiling too. "They're cute," Sam offered.

Iris smiled at the sight of laughing children. Maybe the dogs would be good medicine for everyone. Without another word, she returned to the kitchen.

The entire meal was eaten, every last morsel. It seemed to be a good day for everyone at the boarding house. Before leaving, Missus Reed invited Iris to come to tea the very next day. Iris could hardly refuse, so she accepted.

"See you at four," the elderly woman instructed.

Samuel said his goodbyes as well, and caught Iris by the hand. He bent down and offered a formal kiss on the top. "It is good to see you again, ma'am. Thank you for dinner."

Iris watched him kiss her hand in surprise. It was such an unexpected gesture. "You are welcome, Mister Reed. Truly, indeed. It's good to see a friend from home," she answered with a smile.

David frowned at this statement. Now he might have two men to contend with. He would have to make strides quickly if he was going to win her favor. At least, he consoled himself, he lived under the same roof. Surely that increased his chances. He hoped.

The following morning, both Doctor White and Doctor McCory arrived to check on their patient. After speaking with Hattie and Barney, they were satisfied with her recovery.

"You'll be out chasing those children in no time," Allen McCory promised. "Just don't pick them up for a month, or anything else heavy for that matter."

Doctor White took Barney aside. "No more children. Do you understand? No more."

"Yes sir. I understand," Barney nodded. He wouldn't risk losing his wife ever again.

"Good," the senior doctor nodded. "We'll be back in a week."

Doctor White started to walk down the road, but Doctor McCory lingered behind. "What's wrong, son?" the elder asked.

"I just wanted to speak with Missus Blackheart," he explained.

"Don't get any ideas, son. She's been here for four years and hasn't shown any interest in men. You're wasting your time," he warned.

"Maybe, maybe not," Allen answered. He was bold and brave. It wouldn't hurt to ask. He went up to the door and knocked.

David answered. "Hello Doctor," he greeted. "What can I do for you?"

"I've come to speak with Missus Blackheart. Is she home?" he questioned with determination.

"Yes. Upstairs. I'll get her." David left the young doctor on the porch. He grinned as he went to find the pretty widow. It would be interesting to see how she reacted to him.

"That new doctor is here to see you," he told her. "I think he has ... ideas."

Iris made a face. "Ideas? What does he want?"

"I'm sure he won't tell me," David replied with a smirk. "But I'd guess, it's you he wants." There. He'd planted the idea that would ruffle her feathers, hopefully.

Iris snorted and dropped the sheet in her hands. David watched in satisfaction as her printed cotton skirt swished side to side over her hoops. She was such a lady, even when she was irritated. He longed to hold her in his arms, to kiss her sweetly. He sure couldn't waste time with all these men coming around.

At the door, David overhead Allen inviting Iris to take a short walk.

"I'm right in the middle of chores, Doctor," Iris told him. "Can't you tell me what you need? How's Hattie?"

"Um … she's fine. She will be fine," he stammered. Then he looked nervous. "Will you please come to the porch at least, so I can speak with you privately?" Allen gave David an annoyed glance.

Iris stepped out and closed the door behind her. "Whatever is it, Doctor?"

"I was hoping, Missus Blackheart, that when the church has the dance in a few weeks, that you would do the honor of saving a dance for me?" he blurted.

"Oh," she smiled. "I do plan to be there, Doctor. And I do plan to dance, as much as I can. So, I suppose I can save one for you. Certainly," she nodded.

Allen McCory smiled wide enough to show his teeth. Victory! "Thank you, Missus Blackheart."

"Actually, my name is Missus Picket. Iris Picket," she corrected him.

"Are you really married?" he gulped.

"No. I mean, I was. He died in the war. It's a long story," she rambled.

"Iris. That's very pretty. Where are you from?"

"Lexington, South Carolina."

The doctor's brows furrowed. "How did you get transplanted so far from home, with the war? May I ask this, do you mind?"

"I don't mind telling it now. I'm safe now," she began. Iris then explained some of the situation.

"What a story!" Allen declared. "All true, I'm sure." He gave her a smile of assurance. "Well, I'm glad you're here and that you've agreed to give me a dance."

Iris nodded, and spotted a puppy headed to the Montgomery's cabin.

"I'm from Pittsburgh myself," the doctor continued. "Ever been there?"

"No," she answered, forgetting her chores at present. It was rather nice, now that her defenses were down, to have someone show her a little attention.

"Would you like to go? I'd be honored to take you one day," Allen offered.

That was too much. "No, thank you. That's not proper and you know it."

"I know," he grinned sheepishly. "Maybe under different circumstances …"

Inside, David gritted his teeth.

"May I ask your age, Doctor?" Iris questioned.

"Certainly. I'm twenty-four," he answered proudly.

Iris smiled. "You do realize that I'm older than you," she confessed.

Allen grinned and said, "Really? That just makes you wiser, so they say."

Iris laughed out loud at that comment. David was watching from behind a curtain now. He was jealous that Allen was making her laugh. Allen had to go.

"Still want to dance with an old lady?" Iris teased. "There are so many pretty young girls in town …"

"Absolutely!" Allen cut her off. He then went on to say she would be the belle of the ball, no matter who came.

Iris continued her friendly conversation with the likeable doctor for several more minutes.

When she returned to the house, David asked, "What did he want?" Although he knew perfectly well.

Iris shot him a look. "Not that it's any of your business, but he wants a dance with me next week at the church social."

"Do you want to dance with him?" David questioned jealously.

"Honestly David! Yes, I want to dance. I'll dance with many men that night. I want to go have fun. My husband didn't let me go to dances and parties and now I'm free and I plan to enjoy myself," she shot back with anger.

Iris' hands were on her hips as she glared at him. David knew he was on dangerous ground. Timidly, he asked one more question. "Will you dance with me too?"

"If you don't make me mad I will. Don't you act like you own me, David Stoneman. I'll kick you out of this house fast!" she warned. "I have work to do."

David watched as Iris stomped up the steps. It was the first time he had seen her truly angry since she'd slapped him that time in the parlor. He was blowing it. Angry with himself, David decided to take a ride on his horse. When he left, he slammed the door, just so she could hear it.

David returned late that afternoon with a bunch of wildflowers he had found in a field. He decided to apologize and explain that he was jealous. It would be a good way for Iris to know that he liked her. Honesty was the best policy. "Iris?" he asked.

"She went to Missus Reed's for tea," Barney told him from the yard. "Won't be back for a while."

David's shoulders slumped. He would have to wait. Not wanting the flowers to die, he went in search of a vase.

Iris had put on her best spring dress for Missus Reed's tea. It was a lilac colored silk with a ruffled skirt. For some reason, she was actually nervous about going over there. She knew it was Samuel's presence. Without Hattie to help with her hair, Iris had done the best she could, pinning it up in a simple bun. Her blue felt hat with purple flowers and satin ribbon topped off the costume.

The walk to Missus Reed's home only took fifteen minutes. Iris looked up at the sky. It was a bright blue, with thick clouds floating on the horizon. It seemed a perfectly wonderful summer afternoon. When she arrived, Sam opened the door.

"Hello again," he greeted cheerfully.

"Hello, Mister Reed."

"Is she here?" Missus Reed's voice called from the kitchen.

"Yes, ma'am," Sam answered loudly. "Come in," he then told their guest.

Iris entered the quaint little parlor and began to remove her bonnet.

"Grandmother will be out in just a moment," Sam spoke. "Please sit down."

She did so, choosing her favorite settee. Iris waited for Sam to begin the conversation. "How has your day been?" he asked.

"Good, thank you." After an awkward pause, she asked, "And yours?"

"Fine, fine," he replied with a nod.

Missus Reed walked into the room. "Good afternoon Iris. Sorry I couldn't greet you at the door. I was taking some treats out of the oven. They should be cooled in just a few minutes."

Iris smiled at her good friend, thankful that she seemed talkative today.

"I've spoken with Sam about how you two met. Interesting story," Missus Reed began. "Do you think you will go home soon, to your mother?"

"I don't know, ma'am. I'm waiting to receive a letter from her first."

"Sam told me that he is going to stay with me 'till I kick the bucket," Missus Reed said next without batting an eye.

Sam coughed. "I didn't say that!" he protested.

Iris giggled quietly.

Sam looked in her direction. "Truly," he stated. "I just told her that I would stay here as long as she needed me."

"I'm sure you will," Iris answered kindly.

Changing the subject, the grandmother asked Iris, "How is that maid of yours? I heard she had a tough time of it last week."

"Yes, ma'am. She almost died. One baby survived out of the pair and he is doing well. They named him Bo, but they call him B.B., for Baby Bo," Iris informed them.

"Cute. B.B." the lady answered. "And the mother?'

"Mending slowly, I'm afraid. Mister Montgomery spends all his time taking care of their house, his wife and children. I'm afraid I'm left to care for my own home alone. It can be tiring with guests coming and going."

"Is there anyone there tonight?" Sam asked.

"Only Lieutenant Stoneman," she answered. "But he can fend for himself."

"Does he have business here?" Sam wondered.

"Not particularly," Iris answered honestly. "I don't really know why he remains."

"Sure you do, honey," Missus Reed shot back. "He likes you, I'd guess, a lot."

"Missus Reed, really!" Iris spoke with embarrassment.

"Don't act so naive, Iris dear. He has intentions for you. Even I can see that. It's in the way he looks at you. I may be old, but I'm not blind," the lady insisted.

"Now really, ma'am, he's said nothing to me," Iris explained fervently.

"Do you honestly think he would just come out and say it? Men are shy about these things. Isn't that right, Sam?" she asked.

Sam looked at the two women, taking in the thoughts of their conversation. Without expressions, he answered, "Yes, ma'am." Sam was thinking of a picture of Iris with the Lieutenant. He could not see them together as a pair. North and South? They didn't match.

"Whether you know it or not, Missus Picket, you're a good catch for any man in these parts. Now that the war is over, these men will be wanting wives. You're a widow; it wouldn't surprise me if you were married by this time next year. Sooner even."

Iris was annoyed that Missus Reed would say such a bold statement. How dare she make such a general prediction about her life. Iris opened her mouth to respond, but nothing came out.

"Grandmother, I think it's time for those refreshments," Samuel told her. "Why don't I help you with them?" He suggested offering his hand to escort her into the kitchen. He could see the distress on Iris' face. Granny had been too outspoken.

When they returned a minute later, Iris had regained her composure. Missus Reed wouldn't look Iris in the eye. She knew that Samuel must have said something to her, and for that she was grateful. Iris certainly did not want another husband and she most certainly hoped her behavior showed it.

"I think you will like these, Missus Picket," Samuel spoke first. "Grandmother found a new recipe for these strawberry tarts. You're the first to try them."

Iris looked at him kindly. "Thank you. I'm sure they will be very good."

No more was mentioned about husbands or even men in general. Conversation centered around food or the weather or the train schedule. Right before Iris was to leave, a rumble of thunder rolled in the distance.

"Do you want to stay until the storm passes?" Missus Reed asked.

"I should probably try to get home. These storms sometimes last for hours."

"You know you are welcome to stay," Rose Reed offered. "And I'm sorry for before."

"Yes, ma'am. I know. Thank you, but I really should get going." Iris stood and smiled at her host and hostess. "Thank you both for the tea."

"I have a parasol you can use to stay dry," Rose offered. "Wait here. I'll fetch it."

Iris and Sam were left alone in the parlor. Sam whispered to her, "I'm sorry about what she said earlier. She has a bad habit of wanting everyone to be married. She won't mention it again for a while."

"Thank you for intervening for me. I really don't want to marry again."

When his grandmother returned, they both offered her a smile. "You be careful!" Iris was told.

"Yes, ma'am. Thank you."

Missus Reed waved goodbye and called out, "See you Sunday."

Not five minutes after she had left, the rain began to come down lightly. The thunder was closer now and more threatening. Iris quickened her pace. In her mind, she thought about how much Samuel had changed. He seemed much older, and was very reserved. She wondered what the war had done to him, other than his physical injury.

Lost in thought and in a hurry to get home, Iris did not notice the small, wet, smooth stone in her pathway. She stepped on it and lost her balance. Before she could catch a breath, Iris was sitting on the wet dirty ground. Her skirts spread out everywhere, soaking in the rainwater. The parasol had fallen as well and was also covered in fresh mud. Taking a settling breath, Iris pulled herself up. No use hurrying now, she was a mess.

"Isn't that just dandy?" she asked herself out loud. As she started walking again, a streak of lightening cracked overhead. Then, the rains let loose from the sky and poured down like a continuous wall of water. Accepting her circumstances, Iris closed the parasol and let it hang by her leg. She walked home slowly.

After only a minute or two, she heard a horse running up ahead. Iris looked at the edge of the road that curved around some trees. She could see Lieutenant Stoneman, wearing a rain slicker, riding hard in her direction. He pulled up to a stop beside her. "I thought you might be out here," he spoke hastily. "Looks like I came too late. Did you fall?" After that question, he jumped off his horse.

"Yes." She was partially glad to see him, or the horse, at least.

"Here. I'll help you up," he offered. "You can cover up with this." He offered up the rain coat.

"But I'm already soaked. It won't do any good," she protested.

"It will keep you from getting chilled. Or pneumonia," he suggested. "Please take it."

She pulled the coat around her as she sat on the saddle. It was a man's saddle, so she was a little off balance as she held onto the pommel. With both legs hanging to the left, she twister her upper body to stay on.

David took the parasol in hand and led his horse toward the house. He walked in all the mud, getting soaked by the rain as well. Iris said nothing to him, but took note of his kindness. Once they reached her home, he safely deposited Iris on the front porch before leading his horse back to the barn.

Inside, Iris went to the kitchen. She filled several pots with water to heat for a bath, and cleaned her hands as well.

"How can I help?" David offered.

"There's nothing you can do until the water heats up," she replied. "I'm just going to get some fresh clothes." She began to leave, but paused in the doorway. "Thank you for coming for me."

"You're welcome. I felt badly about this morning. It's the least I could do."

Iris made a small noise in her throat and excused herself to go upstairs. She pulled out fresh clothing and set it on her bed. A blue-striped princess dress with buttons all the way down would be very comfortable for the evening. It was simple enough for sitting around the house. Iris also pulled out a fresh petticoat, corset and dry linen pantalets. She would forego the hoop skirt for the layered ruffled petticoat. Once the clean clothes were assembled, she threw them into a basket to keep them clean while she carried them downstairs.

Iris found David working in the kitchen when she returned. "What are you doing?' she questioned.

"Thought I would make supper tonight," he replied honestly.

She held back a grin. "You?" Her eyebrows were lifted in doubt.

"Yes, me. I know a few things about cooking."

Without another word, Iris walked over to test her bath water. It was nearly ready. "What are we having?" she then asked nonchalantly.

"David's surprise," he answered with a devilish grin.

"As long as the surprise isn't possum, or squirrel or something gamey like that," she warned.

David only grinned and continued whatever he was doing. "Just let me know when that water's ready. I'll carry it to the tub for you."

Forty minutes later, Iris emerged from the wash room. A wonderful aroma filled the kitchen. She could hardly believe it. Her table was set with a clean linen, fresh flowers and full dinnerware. "My goodness!" she exclaimed softly.

David looked up from his work. He smiled with pleasure. She was so beautiful, even with wet hair. It hung long and black down her back. He had never seen it hanging down like this before. She didn't wear her hoops either. This was unusual. "Madam, won't you sit down? Supper is almost ready."

Still surprised, Iris sat at her place at the table. David brought over three covered dishes and set them down. He then sat down in his chair. "Let us give thanks," he suggested. "Will you take my hand?"

With a bit of hesitation, Iris put her hand on the table. He took it gently and stroked one of her fingers softly before he began. "Dear Lord, I thank you. I thank you for providing for all of our needs. Forgive us for our anger. Help us to better know your love. Bless this food. Amen."

Iris looked at David's expression. He was watching her, hoping for approval. She quickly pulled her hand away when Missus Reed's words resurfaced in her mind. He has intentions for you, the woman had said. Iris felt butterflies in her stomach.

"What do you think?" he asked.

"Hmm? I'm sorry. What?"

"What do you think?" he repeated. "Chicken and dumplings, green beans and beets."

Without wanting to encourage him too much, Iris answered, "I think I've never known a man who could cook."

David looked up. "Well, I can. Hand me your plate."

When the meal was nearly over, Iris had to admit that he was a good cook. The food had been delicious.

"Where did you learn this skill?" she asked curiously.

"My mother loved to cook. I spent time with her in the kitchen because she gave me handouts and a growing boy is always hungry," he admitted with a laugh.

"Well, it was very good. I thank you kindly for it," she spoke sincerely. David grinned at the compliment.

After a brief pause, he said, "Do you realize that this is the first supper in a long time that we've had alone? I'm glad. I like spending time with you." And there it was, the truth that he liked her. He had to get it out there with so many other men coming around.

Iris only smiled nervously, fearful of where this conversation was going.

"Well, you see, I've been alone for a long time. And I don't want to be alone any more," he confessed. "I'm quite fond of you Iris, and I hope very much that in time, you will grow fond of me too."

Those butterflies were back. Iris smiled thinly, not wanting to hurt his feelings. "Mister Stoneman, I appreciate your feelings and respect our friendship, but that is all that it can be. I do not plan to ever fall in love again. I was much too hurt the first time. I won't open myself up for the same thing again."

David sat quietly in his seat for a few minutes. The room seemed so silent. Iris looked away at anything she could find to rest her eyes upon. David finally cleared his throat. "Don't you get lonely, Iris?" he wondered, daring to use her first name for the second time in this conversation.

"No, not really. I always have people around me and there's so much to do," she replied honestly. "Like dishes." She nodded toward the ones on the table.

"But don't you ever get lonely for love? Don't you want to be loved?" he questioned in pursuit of the truth.

"I don't need a man's kind of love, Lieutenant. Besides, I am loved. Hattie's children adore me. My friends love me. And if my parents are still alive, they love me too."

"Then I stand corrected," David conceded. "I beg your pardon." Then he stood from the chair. "I'll clean the kitchen."

No more was spoken of it that night. David had cleaned the kitchen as promised while Iris sewed quietly in the parlor. Afterward, David went out to the front porch to smoke a pipe. He remained out there until Iris went upstairs to bed. He felt a little sorry for her. She had given up on love. His body ached to hold her in his arms, but sadly, he acknowledged that it may never come to pass. But if she could just get a taste of being cared for, maybe she would change her mind. Nodding to himself, David determined to do just that. He would do his best to love her for the next few weeks. If she still refused him, he would leave, knowing it would only cause him grief if he remained.

10

Less than twelve hours after their shared supper, Iris woke to the smell of coffee brewing downstairs. She wondered if Hattie was feeling better and had come to make her meal. Thinking that David would still be asleep in his room, Iris pulled on her robe and tiptoed downstairs.

"Hattie, you should not be out of bed yet," Iris warned softly as she came around the corner.

David looked up from the table and smiled at the sight of his hostess wearing her nightgown and robe. Her long black hair was braided behind her head and she still had the look of sleep on her face.

"Oh!" Iris spoke out. She turned quickly to retreat to her room.

Iris came back down ten minutes later wearing a printed summer dress with sleeves down to her elbows. Small lace trimmed the openings. Her hair was re-braided and spiraled at the back of her head and held in place with small pearl pins.

"Lieutenant Stoneman," she greeted properly.

"Good morning, ma'am," he returned. "The coffee is ready. Fresh biscuits are in the oven. They should be ready in five minutes."

Iris raised her eyebrow. What was he doing? She silently poured herself a cup of the hot black drink.

David spoke, "I was wondering ... would you mind if I worked in the garden today? It's going to be a beautiful day, no rain, I think. And since I find myself currently a man of leisure, at least for a while more, I would like to work on something productive."

"Suit yourself," she replied nonchalantly. "I plan to walk into town today and see if my mother has sent me a letter."

"You know, you really could use a horse of your own," David suggested. "You are welcome to take mine into town if you wish."

"Thank you, but I think I'll walk. Like you said, it is such a pretty day."

After breakfast, Iris checked on Hattie. Barney was busy trying to keep the children under control while caring for his recovering wife. Hattie was in good spirits, but still in some pain. She would be in bed for a while longer. Iris promised to bring her friend a surprise from the store in town.

Iris set out in a good mood. Her large straw hat shielded her face from the sun. She passed several people on her way to town. Everyone seemed to be out and about today, getting things done. At one point along the road, a group of her young, single friends smiled and waved.

"We were just coming out to your house," Patty explained.

"Yes, we need your help for the church dance," Margaret said with excitement in her voice.

"Will you help us with the decorations?" Bonnie asked pleadingly

"Sure, I guess so," Iris agreed. All these girls were younger, from eighteen to twenty-two, but they were her friends. Everyone her age was married. Although, there were only three other women her age in the whole town.

"Good, we'll be over to your house tonight at seven. We're getting the supplies from the store," Margaret added.

"Will the Lieutenant be there?" Patty questioned. The other girls giggled.

"I'm sure he will be," Iris confirmed.

"Good," Patty answered. The trio giggled again.

"Where are you going?" Bonnie wondered.

"Into town, to see if my mother has written to me yet," Iris replied.

"Good. We'll go with you."

Town was busy because a train was being loaded at the station. People and goods were everywhere. The street was full of wagons and horses, residents and visitors. The four friends watched for a few minutes with genuine curiosity.

"Don't you wish we could just get on that train and go somewhere exciting?" Bonnie asked them. There was real longing in her voice.

"Yes! I would love to travel," Margaret agreed. "It would sure be better than staying in this little mountain village."

The other friends nodded. Iris did not share their longings. She liked it here. Life was quiet, safe and good. Besides, she had done her fair share of traveling and had seen plenty of the country.

"What was it like, Iris? Traveling all the way up here from down south?" one friend asked.

"It's a long story, girls. Maybe tonight I can tell you some of it," Iris replied. Her three friends were thrilled at the thought.

"Oh good!" Patty exclaimed softly. "Look, there's Mister Reed."

"Oh my. He is so handsome," Margaret sighed.

"You know who else is handsome?" Bonnie asked. "That new doctor."

"I predict that one of us will marry either the Lieutenant, Mister Reed, or the doctor before Christmas," Patty declared merrily.

"Oh!" the girls echoed, then followed it with a giggle. Iris just watched, not really a part of this conversation. She thought these girls were acting mighty silly over men.

"Look, he sees us," Margaret declared in a whisper. She attempted to regain her composure. She waved in a ladylike manner at the gentleman.

Iris watched as Sam waved back.

"Oh my gosh, he's coming over here!" Bonnie gasped in a low voice.

"Hello, ladies," Sam greeted politely.

"Hello, Mister Reed. Good morning," the three younger women spoke in turn.

Sam turned to Iris. "Missus Picket, did that storm catch you yesterday?"

"Yes. I'm afraid it did."

"If I had a horse, I would have come for you. But I'm afraid there was nothing I could do. I can't even run and catch up to you," he admitted, tapping on his bad leg.

"That's quite all right. The Lieutenant came for me," Iris answered, not noticing the look on her friends' faces.

"That's one of the reasons I'm in town today. To get work going so I can buy a horse. I'm going to start cutting timber up in the hills. That's the only business I know," Sam told them.

"Mister Reed, how will you get up there if you don't have a horse?" Margaret asked.

"I can still walk," he answered.

"But Mister Reed, how will you get the logs down?" Patty wondered, trying to get him to speak with her too.

"I won't bring them down until there's a buyer. Then I'll have money for a team of horses."

"I'm glad for you, Mister Reed," Iris told him sincerely. She was glad he was getting his life back.

Sam smiled. "You'll have to guard yourself next time you come over for tea. I won't be there and you never know what grandmother will talk about," he teased.

Iris grinned. "Where will you be?"

"I'm camping out in the woods while I get this lumber cut. I won't be back in town until the church dance."

Iris' friends smiled. "Oh do you plan to be there?" Margaret asked boldly.

"Yes, I do. I promised my grandmother that I would be her escort," he answered with a smile.

"Oh," Patty let a little disappointment escape her lips.

"However, I'm not much of a dancer any more, so I'm afraid I wouldn't be good company for any of you young ladies. You will want to dance and spin," he explained. "I will see you all there though. Now, if you would excuse me please, I have some letters to mail."

"I'm headed that way myself, to see if my mother has written yet," Iris explained. "Bye, girls. See you tonight."

Iris waved to her friends as she headed off with Sam to the post office. "What happens tonight?" he asked.

"We are making decorations for the dance. They asked me to help."

"I don't know why grandmother asked me to take her. She knows I can't dance any more. I'll have nothing to do there but feel self-conscious. I doubt any of those girls would want to dance with me any way. I limp like an old man. No good and broken," he concluded pitifully. He glanced at Iris apologetically. "Sorry, I had no one else to tell."

Iris smiled to reassure her friend. "You are wrong, Mister Reed. There are several girls who would dance with you. I would," she confessed kindly. Then she patted him on the arm before stepping into the building.

"Any letters for me, Mister Woolworth?" Iris asked.

"Hello Missus Blackheart, I mean, Picket," he corrected. "Yes. You have one from South Carolina."

"My mother!" Iris shouted joyfully. "Thank you, sir," she told him quickly. She snatched the letter from his hand. "Excuse me, gentlemen." Then she ran outside to read the letter in private.

Dear Iris. We are so elated to hear from you. Tom and I are alive, having survived this horrid war. Our beloved home in Charleston was destroyed, however, and we have picked up the pieces and found a small house on the outskirts of town. Tom's leg was shattered, and was removed by a field surgeon. He now gets about in a wheeled chair, but his spirit is remarkably good, considering all. We heard about Johnathan and are glad his fate is sealed. Sounds like you have fared well these last several years. We worried about you and prayed for you each and every day. As soon as we can get the money, we will purchase tickets and come to see you. With Tom injured, it is hard for him to work. Most of the servants are gone too, we only have one now. Anytime you want to come home, you can. We have a two room house, just in case you return one day. Please continue to take good care of yourself and write to us again soon. Love always and forever, Mother and Tom.

Iris smiled and held the letter to her heart. They were alive! But not in very good condition by the things her mother shared. From the sound of it, they didn't have very much money. Iris had some. She would send it to them, or better yet, take it to them. She wondered if they would ever consider living with her. She had the bigger home, the better living. She would have to give it all some thought overnight.

"How is she?" Sam's voice asked from a few yards away.

Iris spun around. "They are alive!" she answered happily.

"Good. I'm so glad."

"They aren't doing well though. It seems Tom, that's my stepfather, he lost a leg and now is in a wheelchair. Their fine house was destroyed and now they live in a little two room cottage outside of town. Would it be safe to send them money, do you think?"

Sam frowned. "I don't know. It depends on who's in charge of the mail service. Could be Union soldiers are going through everything. If you send money, they might take it. I just don't know," he told her honestly.

Iris thought for a second. "Do you think it would be safe for me to travel home?"

Sam looked at her carefully. "Well, it's never a good idea for a woman to travel alone … but you did it once before."

"I wasn't alone though. I had Hattie with me. She can't go this time though, not that she would. And Barney can't go, he needs to stay home too. I would have to go alone this time. But if I could get down there, I could bring them back here. They would have a nice home to live in," Iris spoke her thoughts aloud.

"Would you want an escort?" he offered. "I could go with you. But I can't leave until after the church dance. By then, I could sell some lumber and have the money."

"But that money is for your horses. I wouldn't ask you to do that," she told him while shaking her head. "Besides, it wouldn't be proper for us to travel together, Mister Reed. You know that."

"You and I both know it wouldn't be proper under most circumstances, but we could charade as brother and sister, if you really want to go. Or cousins. People would believe us since we both have southern accents. Just think about it, and let me know," he suggested.

"Thank you, Mister Reed. I will consider it," she agreed. "I must write back to her right away. Please excuse me."

Sam waved farewell. How great it would be to spend some time with her. She was so pretty and kind-hearted. At one time, he would have been interested in finding a wife. But now, Sam felt as though no woman would want him. He had nothing to offer: no money, no home, no security. At least he had enough health to work. Sam decided to leave today to go into the woods and begin cutting the trees.

Iris hurried home while her mind spun with future possibilities. David was in the garden when she arrived.

"You look happy," he told her.

"I am! My parents are alive. I got their letter today," she gushed, waving the paper in the air. "I need to talk with you about it, too. I need your advice."

David dropped the hoe and walked over. "Want to sit on the porch?"

Iris read the letter out loud, then told David her thoughts. "Do you think I should send money, or take it myself?"

"I don't think you should take it yourself, that's too risky a trip. However, my father could certainly help. Remember, he owns a bank. He has connections and we could open an account in your stepfather's name. Then he could take out what he needs," David explained simply.

Overcome with excitement at this idea, Iris jumped up and gave David an unexpected hug. "Oh, David, that would be so wonderful! Can we do that?"

David returned her hug with his heart soaring. "Of course we can. I can wire Father today."

"I can't get the money to him today," Iris cautioned. "It will take me a few days to get it. I have some cash, but I can get more if I sell some things. I want to give them three hundred dollars. That should be more than enough to keep them fed and sheltered for a while. Oh David, thank you so much for helping." Iris stopped talking for a moment to wipe a tear. She was just overcome with emotions. "I have to go write them a letter and tell them what we're doing. I want to invite them to come live here too. I don't want to leave this house. It's a good life here. I want them to come up."

"I'll go into town now and send a telegram to Father," David replied. He watched Iris rush inside, lost in her own thoughts.

Dear Mother and Tom, how good it is to know you are alive! I was so eager to hear from you, but am saddened to learn your news. Your lives can't be easy now, as mine wasn't a few years ago when you helped me escape. Now I can help you. My dear friend Lieutenant Stoneman's father owns a bank. He is now opening an account for you in Charleston with funds I will deposit. I hope that $300 will help. I want to invite you both to consider moving north to live with me. I own a large home with plenty of rooms. You could live comfortably. There is even room *for your servant. Please consider taking this money to purchase passage to Baltimore or Philadelphia, as either is a good port to begin the train journey inland to Williamsport. If you need me to return to assist, please let me know. Your loving daughter, Iris.*

When the letter was finished and addressed, Iris decided she would take it to town right away. Maybe it could go out on the train this afternoon. Also, she could stop by Mister Harris' shop to see if he would buy any of her jewelry. If not, Iris knew she would have to make a trip to Harrisburg. She had only just over one hundred dollars in cash. She had to get two hundred more to pay Mister Stoneman. Iris picked through her jewelry basket. There was quite a bit left to sell. It would be worth it to help out her parents, and possibly bring them to Williamsport. Just as Iris was stepping off the front porch to walk into town, a wagon load of people arrived wanting lodging.

"Howdy, ma'am," the man greeted. His wagon was full of older boys and girls. "Might you have rooms for us tonight?" he asked. "A young woman in town told me you rent them out."

Iris' shoulders fell. She would not be able to go into town now. But, at least her home would be full tonight. That meant more money for her parents, and less jewelry she would have to sell.

"Certainly sir. I've two rooms open. And a wash room too, so the children can get clean."

The man tipped his hat. "Thank you kindly, ma'am. We've been on the road for near ten days now. We could use some washing and a good meal." The man turned around to the group of young people in the back. "Everybody out," he instructed.

Boys and girls, mostly boys, from the ages of ten to fifteen climbed out. Each one carried a small bundle. Iris wondered where they were from, but knew she would find out in time. They were dirty and looked sad.

"Sir, there is a stable in town where you can keep your wagon, or you are welcome to let it remain here. However, I have very little shelter for your horses."

"Oh, that's fine, ma'am. These here horses are used to bein' outside," he answered with a little laugh. The man pulled the wagon off the road and to the side near the trees. A team of three boys hurried over to unhitch the team. The others gathered around the porch and stared at Iris.

"Where are you children from?" she asked.

One of the older boys answered, "All over, ma'am. We're war orphans. Mister Young there, he's a real God-like man. Says it's his mission to find us all homes. So that's what he does. Collects us, then finds us a new ma and pa."

"Oh my!" Iris exclaimed. The youngest girl came up and pulled on Iris' skirt.

"I'm from Jamestown, New York," she spoke in a sweet shy voice. "I had some brothers and a sister, but they're gone now. I don't know where they went," she explained with a somber face.

Iris' heart broke for these children. "I'm so sorry for all of you. I wish you all luck in finding new homes. Why don't you come inside and I'll show you your rooms. We can have one for the boys and one for the girls. Since there are more boys, I'll give you the biggest room. Girls, you can have my other very pretty room for yourselves. My hired man will fill a tub. You can all take turns bathing before supper."

The girls were all thrilled at the thought of getting clean. The boys didn't seem to care so much.

"My name is Missus Picket, if any of you need anything. I'll be downstairs most of the afternoon. You are welcome to sit in the parlor as I know you will conduct yourselves like ladies and gentlemen. And, there are two puppies outside who would love to play with you," she told them.

After half an hour, Barney had water heating for the baths and was headed toward town to get more food for supper. Mister

Steven Daniel Young had introduced himself to Iris and paid for the rooms for the night.

"You see," he began, "every child needs a chance to grow up in a Christian home. It's our duty to help those less fortunate. My wife, rest her soul, helped me run an orphanage before the war began. She passed away in sixty-two. I brought on a younger couple to help me run it. It's in Pittsburgh by the way, but since the war, our rooms have been so full! I have to distribute some of the children to make room for more. I take the eldest ones, because they travel better and aren't afraid to leave. I don't know what will happen when I'm gone. You see dear, I'm fifty-five-years-old. But I have to help as many children as I can. Do you think there are any families here who would like to adopt a child or two?" he finally finished.

Iris thought about his question. "I'm not sure. But you could post a sign in town, or tell the preacher and the doctor. They could get word out for you. How many children are there all together?"

"Sixteen, ma'am. Five girls, eleven boys. All between ten- and fifteen-years-old. I'd tell you their names, but I know there's no chance of you remembering all of them. I'm sure you will get to know them tonight though, wonderful children they are. Billy is a bit headstrong being the oldest, he acts tough, but I know he hurts inside like the rest of them. Alex is our oldest girl. Alexandria is her real name ..."

Just then, David returned from town. Iris smiled and introduced their new house guest.

"How do you do, sir?" David greeted, offering a handshake.

"Very well, thank you."

David grinned. "I was wondering where all those children in the yard came from."

"From all over, sir. They are orphans. I'm finding homes for them," Steven explained. He then turned to his hostess again. "May I bother you for pen and paper, ma'am? I would like to make a list of the children and post notice in town."

"Certainly." Iris went upstairs for the needed items, and tapped on the girls' door on her way down. "Ladies, the bath water is ready if one of you wants to come down."

From within the room, she heard a quiet, "Thank you, ma'am."

Downstairs, Iris gave Mister Young the paper and pen, then turned to David. "Will you help me with the bath water?" It was so heavy.

David eagerly followed Iris into the kitchen. As he was carrying the heavy pot to the tub, he asked, "Do you want help with supper tonight? I know this is a houseful and one person can't do it all."

"Oh thank you so much. I was wondering how I would get it all done," she replied gratefully. "David, sometimes, you are good to me."

David grinned on the inside. A compliment? That was a good sign, a step in the right direction at least.

After supper later that evening, Iris and her house guests sat on the porch. Some of the children were inside, talking quietly, while others were outside playing a sporting game of tag. Each was laughing happily, which set well with Iris.

"The children are happy here," Mister Young stated. "Maybe we will stay another day."

Iris was inwardly overwhelmed with the thought of having to cook for nineteen people again. David could see it on her face. He would offer to help again, certainly.

As they were both considering this, Iris' friends, Patty, Bonnie and Margaret, rode up on horseback with their satchels of goods to make decorations for the dance. Iris nearly groaned inwardly. She had forgotten they were coming, and was worn out from the day's chores.

"Having a party?" Bonnie asked jovially.

Iris smiled with fatigue. "No. But my house is full of guests tonight."

"Oh," the young woman paused. "Do you still want to make decorations with us?" Margaret asked. She would be greatly disappointed if she wasn't able to visit with the handsome Lieutenant.

Iris shrugged. "Maybe for half an hour. That's about all I can give."

Mister Young spoke up. "I bet if you asked the girls, they would be glad to help. Four or five more hands would make the work go quickly. What are these for?"

"A church dance, sir," Patty answered.

"How delightful. Those are always fun," he beamed.

Iris excused herself from the porch and went inside with all the women and girls. They set out making paper flowers. Iris learned more about the five orphans, as did her friends. The oldest girl, Alex, was fourteen. Both Betty and Abigail were thirteen. Virginia was twelve and Sara Sue was only ten. The girls discussed themselves for a while, until Iris' friends began to talk about the dance and all the available men.

"I sure hope the Lieutenant asks me to dance with him," Margaret confessed. "I declare, he is the handsomest thing ever walked into this town."

"Well, what about that new doctor? He's mighty handsome too," Patty argued gently.

"That's true. It's just so hard to decide. Then there's Sam. I'd say he's a bit on the thin side, and a little bit dull, but what's a girl to do when there's only three single men in town worth talking about?" Bonnie said to them.

Patty looked perplexed. "What are we to do, girls? There are four of us and only three of them. We have a problem!" All the females giggled except for Iris. She was the matron in the crowd, the oldest, and the only one who had ever been married.

"I'll tell you ladies a secret," she began. "I plan to dance and have a good time, but don't try to match me up with anyone. I want no more husbands, and that's a fact!" she stated adamantly.

"Not ever?" Bonnie asked in astonishment.

Iris shook her head.

"Why not?" Patty wondered. "Are they that bad? Most of the married women I know like their husbands. Don't you ever get lonely for a kiss?"

All the girls giggled again. Iris just rolled her eyes. "Now really girls!" Iris scolded.

David had just happened to overhear her comment from his chair on the porch. He wondered what would happen if he tried to kiss Iris. Maybe it would break this coldness of her heart and put passion in its place. Maybe she would knock him upside his head. He would have to think about it carefully.

From her spot in a nearby chair, Alex blushed. "I've been kissed," she confessed. All attention turned toward the fourteen year old after that. "By a soldier, this past April" she added. "When he found out the war was over, I happened to be standing beside him in town. He whooped and jumped over to me and gave me a big kiss."

All eyebrows went up as the younger girls asked all sorts of questions. Iris just listened quietly as the conversation carried on until just past eight. Finally, her friends told her it was time for them to go. It was getting late and they still had to ride home while there was light in the sky. Everyone said goodbye and they were off.

At eight-thirty, Mister Young announced bedtime. The boys in the yard protested, but complied. All the girls immediately excused themselves, thanking their hostess politely. Mister Young followed the boys upstairs to their room and retired himself. Iris and David were left alone.

"I want to thank you again for helping me in the kitchen tonight," she told him sincerely. "I must confess, if they stay another night, I might fall apart. I'm so tired."

David grinned. "I saw your face tonight, when Mister Young mentioned staying on. Of course, if he does stay, I will help you again. In fact, I'll help with breakfast tomorrow."

Iris grinned a weary smile. "That's an offer I won't refuse."

David was pleased with his progress today. But he wished that he could offer her so much more. That reminded him of something.

"Oh, by the way," he began. "I sent that telegram to my father. He will take money out of my own account to put into one for your parents. Thomas Payton, that's the name I gave him. That was correct, wasn't it?"

"Yes," she replied with her head tilted back and her eyes closed. "I can pay you one hundred and fifty now. I hope to have the other half tomorrow."

"That's fine. I'm in no hurry. Also, I want you to know that I had my father transfer four hundred, not three."

Iris sat up quickly as her eyes flew open. "You did what? David, I don't have that much. I can't get you that much fast," she worried.

"It's a gift," he assured her. "No need to repay, ever."

Iris furrowed her brows. That was one hundred dollars! Men didn't go around giving out that much money without expecting something in return. Good women didn't accept such gifts.

"David, I can't accept it. Thank you, but I can't."

"It's already done," he answered in a calm voice. David could see the concern on Iris' face. "I don't expect anything from you for it either. On my honor, it comes with no strings attached. I just want to help you out, your parents, I mean. It will help them out and I hope will make you happy. My only intention was for your happiness. In fact, I'd do anything for you Iris. I hope you know that."

Iris sat quietly in her chair. Her mind spun with thoughts. He had called her by her first name. He had offered so much money. "I have to think on it, Mister Stoneman," she finally told him. "It's a lot of money."

"I understand," David replied. "Just know, that one hundred dollars is not a lot of money to me. I can spare it. And I'm happy to give it."

Iris listened to the clock tick several times before she stood. "I must go to bed now. Goodnight."

Courteously, David stood as well. He watched her leave the room and hoped that she was not too angry. Sometimes, she was a hard one to figure out. He had sure wanted the extra money to be a good surprise. Maybe, if he kept trying, he could get through to her heart, and win her love.

11

After a fitful night of sleep, Iris woke early. She decided to get a start on breakfast, so dressed quickly in a comfortable cotton dress. She pulled her black hair into a bun and put her feet into quiet slippers. As she tip-toed downstairs to the kitchen, she glanced at the clock. It was only six-fifteen and all was quiet.

First, she put on the coffee. Second, she gathered ingredients for flapjacks and lit the stove. Within minutes, David came downstairs.

"Good morning," he spoke softly.

Iris glanced at him timidly. He carried his shoes in his hands. "I didn't want to wake everyone with my stomping," he offered.

Iris nodded.

"What can I do to help?" he asked.

She pointed to the two tables. "Set them?"

Leaving his shoes on the floor, David walked over to help.

Iris continued to work on the pancakes, and said nothing. She wasn't sure what to say this morning. Of course, she would have to take the money; it was a done deal. But maybe someday, she would repay him. That way, she would not owe him any favors.

David reached into the cabinet for the dishes. Iris did not have nineteen of everything, so the meal would have to be eaten in shifts, as last night's dinner had gone. He set what he could on the tables and went to a drawer for the utensils. Not paying attention however, he reached in and cut his finger on a knife.

"Ouch!" David exclaimed.

"What happened?" Iris asked. Then she saw the blood as he pulled his finger out of the drawer.

"I cut it on a knife. Do you have any bandages?" he asked.

"No. Sorry, I don't."

"No matter. I'll use this." He pulled out a handkerchief and wrapped the white cotton around his finger. Red stain seeped through.

"It must be deep," Iris stated. "I do have ointment. Do you want that?"

"Will it take the pain away?" he asked, trying to make light of the moment. It really was stinging though.

Iris shook her head. "I'm afraid not. But it will help it to heal faster."

David sighed like a little boy, forced to take medicine. "Very well."

Iris went into Hattie's old room and searched for half a minute. She came out with the jar and handed it to David. He carefully smeared the ointment into the cut. After doing so, he began to rewrap the bloody bandage around his finger.

"No, use a clean one," Iris warned. She reached into a small fold of her dress and pulled out one of her own.

"Will you do it?" David asked. "It's easier to tie off with two hands."

Iris stepped forward and wrapped his finger, tying two ends of the cotton wrap securely. "That should do it."

"Thank you, Nurse Picket," David teased.

Iris snorted before going back to her work. "Sometime this morning I have to get into town to mail my parent's letter and stop by the store," she spoke, changing the subject.

"Would you mind my company, if I went with you?" David asked, resuming his task of setting the table. "Or would you rather be alone?"

"If you have business in town, I certainly can't keep you from it," she replied lightly.

Again, David smiled inwardly. More time with her. That had to be good.

Soon after, several of the children came down to eat. Within twenty minutes, the bottom floor was full of people taking turns having breakfast. It was near nine o'clock when Iris was able to leave the house for a short time. Much to David's aggravation, Mister Young's entire group decided to come along for the walk. The leader felt it was a great way to get the youngsters known about town. Maybe, they could find a home if they were seen. The sixteen of them were quite a sight, parading down the center of the street. People did stop and watch with curiosity.

Iris took the letter for her mother and paid for postage. She then went into the store to sell some jewelry. Eagerly, Mister Harris bought much of it. Iris walked out with another hundred dollars. Now she only owed David fifty, if she didn't count that extra hundred. Iris wondered how she could get more money without having to buy a train ticket and travel down to Harrisburg. She would have to think on that one.

When Mister Young decided to remain in town a while longer, David eagerly fell into step beside Missus Picket for the walk home. "So, did you decide to accept my gift?" he asked.

Iris took a breath. "I guess I must, so I thank you for it." She paused, then added, "I sure hope my parents can come up here."

"If they don't, will you go down there?" he worried.

"I don't know really. It's such a long trip. Of course, I'll go if they need me. But Hattie can't go this time and I have the house to run. So, I guess it just depends."

"Then I offer myself as your escort," David spoke sincerely. "I'd be happy to help."

"Thanks, David. Sam Reed offered the same thing. But I won't decide anything until I hear back from Mother again. That should take at least a month."

David's neck stiffened. Sam Reed indeed! "I heard he was starting a lumber business. Guess he won't be around much."

Iris shook her head. "He told me yesterday that he would be in the woods until the church dance. And speaking of the dance, several of my friends will be gravely hurt if you don't ask them for a turn. They've got their eyes on you."

David rolled his eyes. "I can name them too: Margaret, Patty and Bonnie. I assure you Iris, if I don't dance with them, they'll find someone else. I declare those three want to get married so badly, it's written all over their faces. I wager they will be by Christmas too."

Iris grinned. "I believe you might be right on that one. They'll say yes to the first man that asks. I did that once. Horrid mistake."

David kept silent. Iris was obviously still hurting from that first experience.

"You know, not all men are like that, Iris," he championed for his sex. "If I were your husband, I would treat you so kindly. I'd help you cook and clean. We could take walks together, like this one. I'd build us a barn and fill it with wonderful horses to ride. I'd never hit you and would hold you when you were sad." David dared glance in her direction to see her expression.

Iris stared forward with a contemplative look. She kept on walking several steps in silence. "I'm sure you would be good to me, David. I'm just not ready yet," was her simple reply.

No more was spoken on this subject. When they returned home, David set to work on a project outside and Iris went into the house to prepare their noon meal. This afternoon, there was washing to do.

Near four o'clock, Mister Young and his tagalong team came back down the road. Iris could hear the children's noise and came out to the porch. She saw Barney and David pulling logs behind a horse. She wondered what they were up to.

"It's been a good day, ma'am," Mister Young greeted. He smiled and tipped his hat too.

"I'm glad. The children look like they enjoyed themselves."

"Yes indeed! Two of 'em found a home. And two more are under consideration."

"How wonderful. Who?" Iris inquired.

"I found a home, ma'am!" twelve-year-old Virginia shouted with glee.

"Me too!" came a cry from the back of the pack. Iris saw one of the young boys. She did not know his name yet.

"That there's Joe," Mister Young supplied. "A real nice elderly couple, name of Sellers, decided to take them in. They lost one of their sons in the war, it seems."

"Tom. His name was Tom," Iris explained, remembering the kind young man who had helped her and Hattie so nobly when they first arrived.

"Anyway, they said they've got the room and could use some young company and some help around the house being that they're getting up in years. So tomorrow morning, they get a new home."

"Who are the other two?" Iris wondered.

"The boys: Wayne and Joshua, both ten. Family by the name of Byrd. Norman and Elizabeth," the older gentleman supplied.

Iris nodded her head. "They're good folk. They have a farm about three miles out of town. The boys would have plenty of work there. The Byrd's have three children already, but girls."

Mister Young nodded. "Mister Byrd told me he would let me know by noon tomorrow. Once he does, I'll set out south toward Harrisburg with the rest of the kids. I will be needing a room though on my way back. That reminds me, I owe you for tonight."

Iris watched as the man reached into his pocket and pulled out payment for the rooms. She took it with a thank you.

"Billy, Freddy, Max, George, you boys come help us," David shouted at the four oldest. The boys headed over.

"What are you making?" Iris called loudly.

"It's a secret!" David replied with a devilish grin.

"As long as it's not another dog house," Iris warned with a forced scowl.

David chuckled. "It's not."

Iris watched them all suspiciously. Barney was laughing about it too. Iris put her hands on her hips, snorted, then walked into the house to finish dinner.

"May I help you?" a voice asked from behind.

Iris turned to find Alex, the oldest girl. She smiled at her.

"Certainly. Thank you." Alex and Iris set about their work.

"Where are you from?" Iris asked, making small talk.

"A small town about two hundred miles west of here. New Castle. It's north of Pittsburgh," the girl replied.

"May I ask what happened to bring you here?"

"My ma and brother were killed in a house fire before the war. When my pa went off to fight, I went to live with my great aunt and uncle. They don't have much money. When Pa was killed, they sent me away to the orphanage 'cause they couldn't afford me no more," she answered without much self-pity..

"That's very sad, Alex dear. I'm sorry. I'm sure you will find a wonderful family who will be delighted to have you for a daughter."

"I hope so, ma'am."

Iris decided to change the subject. This was too depressing. "Did you know I'm from a town called Charleston way down in South Carolina?" So she then told her all about it.

The following morning, about eleven o'clock, Mister Young returned from delivering both Joe and Virginia to the Seller's home. The Byrd's had not yet come for the two boys, so all the other children had gathered their small bundles and prepared to travel. Missus Rose Reed, Sam's grandmother had heard about the orphans and had brought a large basket of muffins for them to eat on the road. She had also brought them each a little gift. For the girls, there was a new sewing needle and a length of pretty ribbon for their hair. For each boy, there were two pieces of candy and a comb. All the children were delighted with their presents. It broke Iris' heart to see Sarah Sue, the ten-year-old, crying when she climbed into the back of the wagon.

"I don't want to go. I like it here," she told Mister Young.

"I know, dear. You'll like your new home too," he promised.

All the children waved as the horses began to pull away. Just then, a wagon with horses at full gallop came into view at the end of the road. The two people on the front seat were waving and shouting.

"It's the Byrds!" Joshua shouted with glee.

"Horray!" Wayne agreed.

Both boys grabbed their bags and jumped down out of the wagon. When the Byrd's wagon arrived, the boys ran over to their prospective new parents

"Are you gonna take us?" Wayne asked, eager to be taken with his best friend.

"Yes," the man replied. "But you'll have to sleep in the loft until I get a new room built."

"That's fine, sir!" Joshua assured him.

"We don't mind," Wayne grinned.

"Glad to hear it," Mister Young spoke happily. He went over and shook Mister Byrd's hand. They then discussed a little business.

"Boys, I'm so glad to have you," Elizabeth Byrd told the pair. "Your new sisters are at home fixing up the loft for you right now. We are going to have a party tonight with cake."

"Wow! Oh boy!" Joshua exclaimed with euphoric delight. "Did you hear that?" he asked the jealous group in the other wagon.

Within minutes, both wagons had left the yard. Little Noah Montgomery had cried when they left. It had been so much fun for him to have all the children around. There was always someone to play with and give him attention.

"Bye!" he shouted over and over from the road as little tears fell down his cheeks. It broke Iris' heart.

A week later, Iris discovered David's secret project. He was actually going to build her a chicken coop and a barn, of all things. He said she needed her own livestock, at least for butter, milk and eggs. But in his opinion, she should also have some pigs to go along with the cows and chickens. And, she needed shelter for horses. He had also, secretly, written to his father about some business plans.

"I don't have the money or the time for animals, David. You know that. I still owe you fifty for that other transaction," she told him one afternoon.

"I know you're good for it," he replied calmly. "And you will have the money eventually. In the meantime, the barn will be ready and waiting."

She gritted her teeth. He could be so stubborn.

12

The day of the big church dance arrived at last. All of Williamsport was tingling with excitement over the occasion. Iris planned to wear her pretty peach dress. Every woman in town had agreed to bake something and all would share. Mister Harris, the shop owner, had agreed to make enough punch for everyone. Iris only worried he might spike it at some point. The dance was to begin at seven, but Iris and her friends had to get to the church early to decorate. Several men had to go early too because pews needed to be moved.

Hattie and Barney decided to remain at home. Hattie was able to scuffle around the house a bit, but unable to stay up for long.

"We can go next year," Barney told her with a smile.

Hattie did help Iris with her hair though. It was pulled up beautifully along the sides and curled with long ringlets down the back. Iris had not worn her hair in such a way for a very, very long time. It made her feel at least five years younger.

When Iris came out of the house, David was waiting on the porch. He let out a low whistle. "My, my," he said under his breath as he watched the black-haired beauty cross the yard.

Iris saw David sitting in the front chair waiting to escort her into town. He was dressed in fine tan pants, black boots and a white shirt and a black dress coat. He was remarkably handsome, she had to admit. But, she would certainly never tell him that. Instead, she just smiled and said, "I am almost ready, I just have to get the cake."

It was a very pleasant warm night. David held the cake for Iris as they walked.

"You will allow me the first dance, won't you, being that we're such good friends and all?" he teasingly asked.

"You don't give up easily, do you?" Iris returned with a little humor.

He pursed his lips and shook his head. "Nope."

"All right then," she signed. "You can have the first dance."

"Yippee!" David said, skipping around in a little circle like an excited boy.

"Don't you drop that cake!" Iris warned. "Or I won't dance with you at all."

"Yes, ma'am," he answered, straightening up and walking more carefully. Iris grinned as she looked forward.

At the church, David helped the minister and Mister Harris move benches. Iris and her three friends put up their decorations with the minister's wife. Her friends each wore new dresses made just for tonight. Patty's was a pink linen trimmed with delicate white lace. Bonnie's was a lovely pale shade of green, with tiny beads sewn into the bodice. It was considerably low cut, Iris thought disapprovingly. In fact, she was surprised that Bonnie's parents had allowed her to wear it. Margaret's dress was the only one besides Iris' that was made of silk. It was a most becoming shade of pale yellow. Iris knew that Margaret must have had to sell something valuable to purchase this lovely material. Iris also knew that Margaret was twenty-two and desperate to be married before she was an old maid.

"Oh, your dresses are just lovely!" Patty exclaimed to both Margaret and Iris. She looked down at her own cotton dress. "I feel so … so country," she told them.

"No, you look beautiful," Bonnie and the other women assured her.

"My dress is cotton too," Bonnie added. "You know people out here don't expect silk gowns and all. That's for rich city people."

Iris kept quiet, thinking about all the balls and parties she had gone to where everyone wore silk and satin.

"All you ladies look lovely," the minister told them, giving his wife a wink. She wore a modest blue dress with sleeves down to her elbows. It was trimmed in ecru lace that matched the collar. The younger girls giggled. Iris could see David slightly shaking his head at them. It amused her.

Just before seven, the men who played instruments began tuning up outside. The dancing area was actually on the lawn, with benches around for those who wanted to watch. Inside the building were the refreshments on decorated tables. Couples and families began to arrive.

"He's here!" Patty whispered to the girls inside as they finished their work.

"Who's here?" Iris wondered.

"The doctor. Doctor McCory!" she answered.

"Oh!" Margaret and Bonnie both said, walking quickly to the door to get a peek.

"Girls!" Iris scolded. "If you don't stop acting silly, those men won't have anything to do with you."

"Thank you, Iris," the preacher's wife whispered. "Girls, she's right. Don't look so eager."

"Our work is done in here, I'm going out," Bonnie told them.

"Me too!" Margaret replied. Patty followed right behind them.

Tina Louise, the preacher's wife, and Iris collected food from the women as they arrived. At quarter after seven, the music began. David came into the building for Iris.

"Pardon Missus Shepherd, but can you spare Missus Picket for a dance?" he asked.

Tina nodded her head. "Certainly." Inside, she was surprised. No one had expected Iris to truly participate. She had shown no interest in men for over four years. Maybe, Tina hoped, she was finally coming out of her shell.

David extended his hand. "The first dance, Madam?"

Iris accepted, placing her hand gently in his as he escorted her outside. Finding a place in the dance area, they began to step in time. All the townsfolk watched in pleasure as their lovely widow danced with the Lieutenant. Many other couples danced as well. Iris even noticed that Patty had secured a dance with the new doctor. Margaret unhappily danced with a nineteen-year-old farmer. Bonnie danced with her father.

Iris had a grand time. It felt wonderful! She had not danced since the night at the cotton plantation when Sam took her home. And that party had not been fun at all. But this one, was delightful. Not only did she dance with David, but also with the young Doctor McCory, the shop keeper Mister Harris, the senior Mister Sellers and two other men. After thirty minutes, she needed a break.

"I'll just catch my breath now, if you don't mind," she told the next young man who asked. "Ask me again later, please."

Iris went inside for punch, and wondered where Sam and his grandmother were. They should have arrived by now. After taking a slice of lemon cake and getting a glass of punch, she wandered back outside to watch. She noticed then that Rose Reed and her grandson had just arrived. Good. Iris watched as Sam helped the elderly woman down from their wagon. With cane in hand, he slowly came near with Rose at his side. Rose found several of her friends and stopped to talk. Sam continued walking over to where Iris sat on a pew.

"Is this seat taken?" he asked with a smile.

"No. Please do sit," she replied. Once he was down, she admitted, "I was beginning to worry about you both."

"Yeah," he let out a little huff. "We're a little late." He looked over the crowd. "Good turn out," he spoke without further explanation.

"Yes. It seems everyone's here."

"Have you been dancing?" he wondered.

"Yes. And it's been marvelous. But I got winded and had to sit out a few," she confessed. "How has it been for you these last two weeks? Cut many trees down?"

Iris noticed the glimmer in his eyes as he spoke. "Yes, it's been quite good actually." He continued to tell her about how good it had been to be alone and get his thoughts together while working hard. He had been able to prove to himself that he could still do it, even with the bad leg. "I got back in town this morning, and tomorrow will go to the sawmill and find a buyer. If no one here wants it, I'll send a wire into the cities."

"Sounds like you have it all planned out," Iris spoke with encouragement.

"Yes. It feels good to work again. I'll get back on track soon and establish myself. I hope to set up a good lumber company and sawmill right here in town by next summer."

Iris raised her eyebrows. "That sounds exciting, and I wish you well."

Both friends were quiet for a moment. Then Sam said, "You know, things have sure changed in the four years since we first met at the Mayfield's plantation."

Iris nodded agreement.

Sam continued, "Back then, I would have loved to dance with you. Remember, I asked, but you turned me down."

Iris nodded again. "I had to. My husband wouldn't allow me to dance with anyone but him. I would have enjoyed a dance with you though."

"Now, you have the freedom to dance, but I haven't the ability," Sam pouted a little. "I'm very sorry for that. Life can be so cruel."

For the third time, Iris nodded. "Yes, it can."

"That's why we were late coming here," he confessed. "I was feeling sorry for myself because all I can do is watch. I can cut trees, but I can't dance. Grandmother made me come, but I was kicking and screaming the whole way."

Iris turned in disbelief.

"No, it's true," Sam confirmed. "I started to have a little tantrum and she hit me on the head with a pillow and told me to grow up."

Iris snickered at the picture in her mind. "I like your grandmother. She's right. You should get out a little, Sam. Even if you can't dance, you can visit and be good company. Besides, now that you've shaved off your beard, you might even pass for slightly handsome," she teased.

"You're playing with me," he warned, giving her a tender nudge with his elbow.

At that moment, David came over. "Mister Reed," he greeted stiffly.

Sam looked up at the well-dressed officer. "Mister Stoneman."

"Iris, I've come to see if you're rested enough to take another turn with me?" David questioned.

"Well, I hate to leave …" she began, not wanting to be rude and leave Sam behind.

"No, you go dance," Sam told her. "I will watch you."

David furrowed his brow at this comment, but said nothing. He extended his hand to Iris. When they were out dancing, Iris told him, "I hated to leave Mister Reed sitting there alone."

"He'll be fine," David assured her.

"Don't be cold David," she scolded. "He's lonely and feeling down tonight." Just then, Iris spotted Bonnie and Margaret coming out of the church together. "Wait here, I'll be right back," she told David. She pulled herself from his hold and hurried over to her friends.

"Girls, go sit with Mister Reed, please. Take him some punch or something," she suggested.

"What was that all about?" David asked when Iris returned.

"I sent them over to Sam," she replied.

"God help him then," David sympathized. He was jealous when Sam spoke to Iris, but he didn't wish those giggling husband-hunting girls on any man.

"Why do you say that?" Iris asked.

David shook his head. "Because Bonnie's dress is too low and Margaret is way too eager. I danced with them both earlier, as you know. Margaret near talked my ear off trying to be friendly, and I had to look up at the tree tops to keep from looking down at Bonnie."

Iris giggled quietly and tried not to speak loudly. "I'm sorry." She looked over at her two friends who were now on either side of Sam. "And what about Patty?"

"Patty was perfectly sweet, I must say. But at eighteen, she's a bit young for me," he replied honestly.

"Perfectly sweet? She'll like that," Iris said with a pleased smile. Then she turned to look at David straight in the eye. "How old are you?"

"Twenty-nine next month," he answered quickly.

Iris lifted an eyebrow. "So old!" she said in a slow teasing voice. She shook her head as though she disapproved.

"Old enough for you!" he shot back.

"Huh!" Iris answered without another word. They continued to dance in silence. Around nine-thirty, most of the families with young children began to leave. Only the adults remained, about twenty-five people. Iris noticed that Patty had paired off with the doctor. That might be an interesting development. Boy, wouldn't Bonnie and Margaret be jealous. They had both danced with many of the single men tonight, but were not particularly attached to one. Margaret was flirting with them all. Bonnie wasn't actually flirting, but the dress was doing all the talking.

After several more rounds, Iris grew tired. "Let's sit out for a while," she suggested to David. "Will you get us some refreshments, please?"

David agreed and went inside the church. Iris found a seat near Sam. "How are you?" she asked happily.

"Fine, thanks."

"Having fun at all?" she wondered.

He nodded. "I'm finding company. Your two friends make the rounds and check on me every now and then."

Iris smiled. "Good. Where's Rose?"

"Getting punch at the moment, but she found a new friend to dance with earlier. It seems the preacher's father is in town. They've struck up quite a chord."

"How wonderful for her!" Iris cheered.

"Here's the punch," David stated, cutting in to the conversation. He took a seat next to Iris and held a plate of food for them to share. "Hungry?" he asked Sam.

"No. Bonnie and Margaret have fed me all evening."

"Nice girls, those two," David encouraged.

Iris stuck out her elbow to punch David in the ribs. She gave him a warning glance not to say anything more about her friends. David smiled and offered the plate.

Iris took a little food, and gulped her punch in one swig. "David, I'm so thirsty. Would you please get me more punch?"

Not wanting to leave these two alone, David frowned. "If you insist." He went away quickly. Before Sam and Iris could begin another conversation, Rose and her new admirer walked to the bench.

"Iris, Sam, this is Mister Shepherd," she spoke.

"How do you do?" the elderly man asked.

Sam and Iris greeted him kindly and began a conversation. David returned with the punch, which Iris quickly drank again. After a bit, Rose said she was ready to go home. "It's so very late for me," she confessed. Mister Shepherd escorted her to the wagon.

Sam looked at Iris. "May I have a word with you in private, please?"

"Certainly Sam."

David watched as the pair walked toward the perimeter of the lantern light where all the wagons stood waiting. His heart burned with jealousy. What was Sam going to say?

"I just want to thank you for your kindness tonight when I first arrived. I needed a friend and I know you went out of your way to spend time with me and to make sure I was accommodated by your friends," he told her gently.

"Of course, you're welcome. I didn't want to see you alone. You are such a dear friend to me, for what you did for me back home. I owe you so much," Iris spoke sincerely.

Sam looked at this lovely woman with a tender heart. "You owe me nothing, dear Missus Picket. But I will cherish your friendship. May I ... may I give you, would it be too forward to ask you to allow me to kiss you on the cheek. It's something I've wanted to do ever since that night so long ago"

Iris looked at the ground and blushed in the darkness. "Yes, you may."

Sam leaned forward as Iris leaned into him. Sam's warm lips gently pressed against her cheek. When he pulled away, he said quietly, "You are a dear." With that, he turned and helped his grandmother onto the wagon seat. He then climbed up carefully as he kept all the weight off his bad leg.

"Goodnight," he called out to Iris.

"Goodnight," she returned to them both.

David's heart was racing with jealousy. He had seen her lean into Sam for what he assumed was a kiss. As she came into the light, he could also see the smile on her face and a slight blush in her cheeks. He would be so crushed if her heart went to someone else.

Iris gave David a smile. "Let's dance," she suggested. Her heart was light. She had enjoyed Sam's kind compliments and his affection, if truth be told. David took her into the center of the dancing area and spun her around to the music. At the end of the first song, Iris' head began to throb.

"David, I don't feel good," she told him.

"What happened? You were fine five minutes ago," he said with a little sarcasm.

Iris put a hand up to hear head. "I know. I felt great a minute ago. But all of a sudden ... I don't."

"I'll get you a drink," he offered, seeing that she was looking suddenly pale.

He was back in half a minute as a small crowd gathered. David handed her the cup which she drank down quickly. Margaret came over and fanned her friend. Bonnie brought a cool, wet cloth for her face.

"What's wrong?" Patty asked, coming over with the doctor.

"Missus Picket, let me see your eyes," the doctor ordered gently.

Iris opened them, squinted, and closed them again. "No. My head hurts," she spoke weakly. "And my stomach ..."

Just then, Bonnie's father shouted out. "Come back here, young man!"

All heads turned to see the nineteen year old farmer running away with an empty bottle of rum in his hand.

"He spiked the punch!" Margaret shouted.

"Oh!" Iris moaned. She'd had three cups in fifteen minutes.

"I'll take her home," David told the crowd. "Some fresh water will help dilute it. She'll be all right."

"You can take my horse," Allen McCory offered.

"Thanks, Doc."

Allen ran to fetch his horse. Patty, Margaret and Bonnie could not believe what had happened to their friend. She was drunk! When Allen returned, David pulled himself far back into the saddle, then reached down to get Iris. The doctor helped push her up while David pulled. In less than a minute, they had her situated just behind the pommel with her legs hanging over one side. The hoops under her dress made it stick up in a most unusual fashion. Iris' head was slumped over toward her knees. David held her up by leaning his chest against her shoulder and bracing his arms around her body.

"Goodnight, everyone. The dance was real fun," he told them. He nodded toward the preacher, assuring him that Iris would be safe. He then turned the borrowed horse toward home.

It was a quiet night. Stars twinkled in the black sky above and a comfortable breeze blew through the trees. David was quite content with his current situation. Of course, he knew what considerable discomfort Iris was currently feeling, he had been there himself a few times. However, he was delighted with the fact that his arms were around her waist and she was leaning against him. He could feel her weight and it felt good. He could also smell the soap from her last bath. Letting the horse lead, David savored every second.

"We'll get you home, honey. You'll feel better soon. I know it feels bad," he spoke quietly in her ear.

Halfway there, Iris felt her stomach heave. "Stop!" she cried out.

As soon as he pulled the reins, Iris slid down and dropped to her hands and knees. Half a second later, the contents of her stomach came pouring out onto the road. David jumped down too and put a hand on her back.

"Don't ... watch ..." Iris whispered when the first wave ended.

"I won't." He backed away, taking the horse with him. He would give her some space for privacy. Iris was sick twice more, then began to cry.

"Are you done?" David questioned with real concern.

"Yes," came her faint reply. Iris sat in the middle of the road with her beautiful dress all in the dirt. She was mortified! She felt horrible and mortified, so the tears came out.

David walked over and put a clean handkerchief in her hand. "You'll feel better now, and once you get a little sleep," he promised.

"I'm so embarrassed," she whimpered.

David reached to help her up. "It's not your fault. You've nothing to be ashamed of. The guilt rests with the farmer. I've a good mind to go tan his hide tomorrow."

Iris cried softly as they made their way back to the horse. "You might be more comfortable if you sit behind me," David suggested. "Think you can hold on?"

Iris nodded in the dark, but they were close enough for David to see her reply.

David pulled himself up first, then took his boot out of the stirrup. "Don't sit side saddle," he warned. "You'll fall off."

Lacking the energy to argue, Iris took his hand and allowed his strength to pull her into place. She swung her leg over the horse's back and planted herself firmly behind David's back.

"Well done," he complimented. Then with a small noise, he set the horse to walking again. Without being told, Iris put her arms around his waist and held on. Exhausted from getting sick, she rested her head between his shoulder blades. He was a firm pillow. Neither spoke a word the rest of the way home.

When David pulled into the yard, Iris was almost asleep.

"Iris, we're here," he announced. "I'm going to slide off, then reach for you. Keep yourself upright for a few seconds more."

It was not done gracefully, but Iris did manage to fall into David's arms. He looked down at her face. Her eyes were closed again.

"My stars, you're pretty!" he uttered before placing a tender kiss on her forehead. Amazingly, she did not protest. In fact, she was quite limp in his arms. Mustering his own strength, David scooped the woman into his arms and entered the house. Upstairs, he placed her gently onto her bed. She was out cold.

He lit a lamp, then debated what to do. He could at least remove her shoes. Once he did that, he thought about the corset. His sisters had always complained how tight they were. One could hardly sleep comfortably in one, they had said. Determining his next action, David forced himself to do only what was necessary for her to breathe. He rolled Iris onto her side and unlaced the back of the dress. Really, she needed a new maid. Once he could get to the corset, he simply loosened the stays. In her sleep, Iris took a deeper breath. David could see the soft white material of her chemise which separated his fingers from the bare skin on her back. He withdrew his hands from the lacings, but allowed his eyes to caress the skin across her neck. How beautiful she was. David just could not imagine how her husband could have been so cruel. If only she would give him the chance to prove his ever growing love. Maybe, maybe …

13

The sun had been up for over two hours when Iris came downstairs the next morning. David sat at the kitchen table writing letters when she entered in a blue dress. She gave him a look of complete humility.

"Good morning," he spoke calmly. "May I offer you some coffee? It's hot and strong."

She nodded in appreciation and sat down beside his chair. When he slid her the mug, she took a drink without looking him in the face.

"How are you feeling?" he asked.

"I ... I just want to say thank you, for everything you did last night. For taking care of me," she offered. "And for putting me to bed." She paused before adding, "And for loosening my dress. I assume that was you. I did sleep soundly. Please, let's not mention it to anyone."

"You have my word," he assured her.

Iris took another sip of the hot drink. "You are good to me, David." Her eyes watered, but did not spill over with tears. She had so much to think about. Allowing herself to fall for him seemed so frightening. But her heart was torn and confused. She did not trust herself at all.

Two weeks passed with relative peace. Iris was more quiet than usual, but nothing was really wrong. David continued to work on the barn and kept his word about that night. Several guests came through town and slept at the boarding house, so Iris was busy inside. The pair only spoke in the evening, and made small talk about the day.

Hattie was up and about now, but was kept busy with three children. Barney handled the hard work from sun up to sun down. Over and over he proved himself to be a good and worthy man.

Within those two weeks, Patty and Doctor McCory announced their engagement, Sam Reed returned to the woods, and Iris received another letter from her mother."

"They're coming!" Iris called as she entered her yard. Barney and Hattie came out from their cabin to see what was happening.

"What?" Hattie questioned.

"My parents, Hattie. They are coming here in August!" she answered gleefully. "I'm so excited!"

Hattie and Barney smiled. David walked over too. "That's great," he told her.

Iris nodded. "She mentioned you in her letter," she told David. *"Tell Mister Stoneman how kind it was for his father to open the account for us. I cannot begin to tell you what it meant to us,"* she read. "That reminds me, I still owe you fifty dollars. I'll have it by the end of the week."

He just nodded.

"I have to go get things ready," Iris nearly giggled. "There's so much to do." She hurried inside, eager to prepare a room.

The following day, David received a letter from his father. He read it carefully, and considered its contents. That night, when he and Iris were alone, he made a confession.

"Iris, I want to tell you something," he began.

She looked up from her embroidery.

"I wrote to my father several weeks ago, telling him how much this town needs a bank. I plan to open one this fall, once your barn is finished."

"You do?" she gulped. "A bank?"

"Yes. But there's more," he hesitated. "I won't do it without your blessing. I know I have nearly outstayed my welcome in your home and must soon make a decision. People are beginning to talk, about us. I too, feel that our friendship has grown. I hope ... I do hope you have some positive feelings for me. I know you care a great deal about Sam Reed. I won't get in your way if he is who you want, but I want you to know and understand how great and deep is my love for you. I will leave it up to you, whether I am to return home or if I am to stay here and pursue our friendship further."

Iris was stunned. Speechless. She stared at him oddly, in a sort of overwhelmed shock. In her heart and mind she thought about David and how she truly felt about him. He had been with her since the end of April. It was now nearly July. Over these last two months, he had, somehow, melted away the thick ice over her heart. With the protective layer gone, that fragile organ was now exposed to real feelings. She did care for him, deeply. It had snuck up on her without her knowledge. It wasn't until now, at the thought of losing him, that she realized how much she needed him. Oh God! She was in love!

Her gaze went up to his. The unspoken connection was made. Iris opened her mouth to speak. A small whimper came out.

"Don't leave me." Emotions got the best of her as her eyes filled with tears.

David smiled. "Really? You want me to stay?" he asked. He saw the tears. Was this real? Was she weeping for him? Oh how he hoped ...

Iris nodded and gulped back fear.

David slid closer and reached for her hand. "Don't cry, Iris. Please don't cry."

She sniffed and wiped at the water on her face with her free hand. David offered his handkerchief then bent down on his knees to look into her face.

"Iris?"

Forcing herself to get control, she returned his glance.

"I love you," he spoke earnestly. "I love you so much."

More tears fell as her heart gave up completely. Iris leaned in and rested her forehead on his.

"I love you too," she dared to whisper.

David scooped Iris into his arms as he lifted them both to stand. He held her tightly and placed several kisses on her head. Once her weeping stopped, and she simply embraced him, David pulled back.

"Iris, I want you to marry me," he spoke. "And I promise, this time, you will never regret it. Will you have me?"

She nodded and smiled. "Yes. Yes I will."

David leaned in and placed a gentle kiss on her lips. The energy between them was awakened, sending adrenaline through their veins. Iris heard her heart pounding like a drum. Her arms held to his body with desperate yearning. What was once dead within, came alive. Her heart was full of love for him. It made her mind giddy with delight.

Finally, they released. Iris smiled and blushed with joy. David grinned with satisfaction. Her heart was his at last.

"I have a ring for you upstairs," he confessed. "Be right back."

She watched as he left her side. It had all happened so fast. She was still in a daze. But, she was happy. David returned and placed a lovely ruby ring on her finger.

"You make me very happy," he told her. "I will endeavor to do the same for you."

Iris continued to smile. The ring was beautiful. "Thank you," she mouthed.

"I do have a wedding band to give you when we're married." David smiled at his future bride. Then a thought went through his mind. "I'll have to move out until then."

Iris nodded. It would not be proper for him to remain beneath her roof now that they were engaged. "Where will you go?" she questioned.

He shrugged. "Don't know really. Maybe Missus Reed's house. She has that extra room when Sam is gone. I'll have to scoot home too, and collect a few things. The barn will be finished in a week. I'll probably go home then, but just for a few days. Where would you like to go for our wedding trip?"

"I don't know. Can't we just stay here for a while? I want to spend some time with my parents before I leave them again."

"Very well," David agreed. "I assume you will want to wait until after they arrive to be married. I need to tell my family too. They will all want to come out."

"When do you want to be married?" Iris questioned shyly.

David looked at her lovingly. "As soon as possible, of course."

Iris thought about it briefly. "My parents should be here by the second. Can we marry on the fourth?"

So it was set. David and Iris were to be married August fourth. He went to stay with Missus Reed for the week, but worked on the barn by day. When the new couple announced their engagement in town, no one was really surprised. The pair was a good and natural match. Margaret and Bonnie were beside themselves with jealousy though. David also announced his plans to open a bank.

One night, Sam returned from the woods to find David sitting in his parlor. The two struck up a conversation, and before long, a business deal. Sam was to be David's first loan because he was investing in the younger man's lumber business.

"I'll be needing lots of lumber myself," David admitted. "There's the barn, then the bank." Right on the spot, he gave Sam three hundred dollars. The papers were drawn on Rose's parlor desk. Sam was overwhelmed with the thought of establishing his business so much sooner than he anticipated. The men shook on the deal.

David sent a telegram to his parents the same day Iris ordered silk for her wedding gown. Back at home, the room for her parents was ready.

The day came for David to leave on the train. He kissed Iris quickly at the depot and they waved goodbye.

"See you soon," Iris called out. She was sad to see him go, but knew she could stay busy until his return. Walking through town, she noticed several men hammering posters onto trees and store fronts.

"We'll put on a good show," she heard one say. Another man tipped his hat in her direction. She smiled briefly and continued walking. There were three woman and four men in the group. Iris wondered who they were. Several of the townsfolk crowded near.

"A theatrical group," the minister's wife announced. "Oh my!"

Iris had never seen a play. It might be fun to go watch. "When is the show?" she asked one of the women.

"Tomorrow, my dear."

"Good," Iris spoke. "I will come." She said goodbye to Tina and walked home.

Not thirty minutes later though, and the entire troupe entered her front yard. They had a horse drawn wagon in tow.

The tallest man stepped forward. "We were told you had rooms to rent?" he questioned.

"Yes, I do," Iris confirmed. "But only three."

"That suits us fine. We need them for two nights. Allow us to introduce ourselves. We are the Philadelphia Acting Troupe," he spoke with a bow. He then began to name everyone. "This is Wilamena Smith." Iris watched as the woman nodded her head.

"Then Daniel and Lucinda Bloomsburg." They nodded their heads as well.

"George Wright, Nathan Hawkins Hall, Clara Ackley, and I am Scott Dorsey Brown."

"Glad to meet you all. I am Missus Picket."

Iris settled her guests into their rooms and returned to the kitchen. Hattie was able to help her now, thank goodness. Baby Bo hung in a sling against Hattie's chest. It freed her arms to work. Barney watched the other two. It was a fun and entertaining night for Iris. The troupe acted out several scenes as they practiced in the parlor. They even purchased the old wigs Iris had used during her escape north.

Apparently word of the actors spread through town quickly. The next morning, Margaret and Bonnie arrived with baskets in hand.

"We wanted to bring you these special loaves of bread we baked," Margaret told her, looking past Iris' should and into the house.

"Do come in Margaret dear, Bonnie," Iris told them. She knew good and well they just wanted to meet the actors. Iris introduced them one by one. Then her friends, full of curiosity, barraged the newcomers with questions.

"Oh, I can hardly wait for tonight," Bonnie stated. "How exciting! What fun the show will be."

"Will it be in the church?" Margaret wondered.

"No. Your preacher wouldn't allow it," Scott Brown explained. "We will have it outside, under the stars."

That evening, the town was bustling with excitement. Everyone, it seemed, was coming out for the play. It was Shakespeare. The actors had erected a makeshift backdrop by hanging rope and sheets between two trees. Their trunks full of costumes and props were opened and ready for use.

Sam and his grandmother sat next to Iris. Sam congratulated her on the engagement.

"I won't say I'm not jealous," he confided. "But I am very happy for you both."

The entire evening was a success. The play was well acted, with shouts and cheers from the crowd. Everyone had enjoyed a good night's entertainment. It was late into the wee hours of morning before Iris and her guests were quietly settled into bed. She could still hear them talking softly in their rooms when she fell asleep.

"I can't believe it's so late!" Iris told herself as she hurried. It was nine the next morning and she had just awakened. Breakfast had to be made, but thank goodness, all the actors were still asleep.

By eleven, everyone had eaten and the troupe was headed to the train station. They were moving on to the next town. Iris pocketed the money they had given her and set about cleaning the rooms.

Later that afternoon, there was trouble. Margaret's parents drove their wagon into the yard in a terrible hurry.

"Have you seen Margaret?" her mother questioned. "Did she come here this morning?"

Iris frowned. "No, ma'am. I haven't seen her. What's wrong?"

"She left! She left with those actors!" the worried mother replied close to hysterics.

Margaret's father put his arm around his wife. "There, there dear. We will find her."

The man glanced up at Iris. "Margaret told us this morning that she was going into town to get something from the store. Several hours later, we found this note." He held up a sheet of paper. "She told us she was going away with the troupe and that she would write to us every week so we would know she was safe. We're quite distressed, as you can imagine. Do you know where the actors were going next?"

Iris shook her head. "No, sir. They only told me that they were going on to the next town. Honest, that's all I know."

Margaret's father nodded his appreciation. "Thank you, Missus Picket. We will send some telegrams and find them." His voice was solemn and sad. With his wife by his side, he turned the wagon and headed back into town.

As word spread, the townspeople were greatly surprised to hear that Margaret had left. It was almost scandalous and her parents were so ashamed. After some search, they located the troupe in Allentown. When they went to bring their daughter home, she refused. Margaret was enjoying her exciting new life, and was over waiting around for a husband. She told them she was going to make her own future, travel the country, and have an adventure. Bonnie, most especially, was saddened by the loss of her friend. With both Patty and Iris engaged, and Margaret gone, Bonnie was left alone.

A week later, Iris received a telegram from David. "Returning July 24 with family. Train arrives 7:30 pm. Meet me. Yours, David," she read out loud.

Iris was glad he was coming home in two days. How nervous she would be to meet his parents. She wondered what they and his sisters would be like. Iris decided to make their rooms especially nice, with cut wildflowers and extra lace doilies. She also needed to get with Hattie and plan some special meals. Then they would have to do the shopping.

It was while Iris and Hattie were in town that Mister Young returned with a near empty wagon. Alex sat on the front bench at the driver's side. The expression on her face showed the weight of the world. Her hope was lost; she was dejected.

Iris waved and said, "Hello."

Mister Young answered with a cheerful greeting. "Good day to you, Missus Picket. We're returned from our journey."

"I'm glad to see you again," Iris told them both. "Alex, hello dear."

Alex gave Iris a sad smile.

"Are you on your way to my house?" Iris questioned.

"Yes, ma'am, we are. Would you like a ride?" Mister Young offered.

"We are not quite finished sir," Iris explained.

He nodded. "Alex and I can wait."

Iris smiled. "Thank you. Hattie and I will only be a few minutes more. Alex, would you like to help us?"

The girl shrugged, having lost interest in just about everything in life.

"You go on now," Mister Young encouraged.

With a heavy sigh, Alex climbed down. Iris could read the gloomy depression in the girl's eyes. Alex's clothing was covered in dust from weeks of travel. Her face was thin and the faded cotton bonnet she wore had a large hole in the seam. Iris wondered what had happened. Maybe, the girl was just sad because she was the last one left. No doubt she felt unloved and unwanted. Those were feelings Iris could relate to.

"Alex, we need your help to decide on the food," Iris explained. "We are going to have a lot of guests at the house over the next few weeks. There's so much to do. I remember that you were such a help last time in the kitchen. What's your favorite meal? Let's buy the supplies and make it. Dessert too. What's your favorite?"

Alex was quiet for a moment. She had dreamed of being able to have a feast. If only ...

Hattie looked at Iris, then at Alex. "You sick, honey?" she asked.

Alex shook her head.

"What do you want to eat then?" Hattie repeated.

"I like fried ham," Alex finally answered.

"Very well. I like that too. Let's get some," Iris told her.

"What else?" Hattie wondered.

"Mashed potatoes and fresh bread?"

Iris and Hattie nodded.

"Sounds good," Hattie grinned. "What about something sweet?"

Alex bit her lip as she stared at the two women. "I like blueberry pie," she answered in a quiet voice.

"And so you shall have it," Iris promised, wanting to make this sad girl happy again.

"We can make it this afternoon," Hattie added. "It's my husband's favorite too."

And so the shopping was completed. Mister Young carried the women and their goods back to the house in his empty wagon. Iris was glad for the ride, they had bought quite a bit and this saved her the trouble of having it all delivered. Alex, Mister Young and Barney helped unload the groceries.

Once that was done, Iris turned to the dusty orphan. "Alex honey, would you like a nice bath?"

Alex nodded. "Yes, ma'am."

Iris and Barney set up the bath tub and filled it with lukewarm water. Iris gave Alex a bar of honeysuckle soap and a brown sea sponge for scrubbing.

"Head to toe," she told the girl. "And I'll see if I can find you something clean to wear."

Upstairs, Iris riffled through her trunks. Surely there was something here the girl could use. At the bottom of the second one, Iris pulled out a long forgotten white cotton print. There were small green leaves on this everyday house dress, and a pretty green ribbon sash at the waist. It was perfect for Alex and with a few tucks here and there, it would fit her well enough. Iris grabbed an extra ruffled petticoat too. It would help the skirt stand out, as was the fashion, and help it fit better too. Iris grabbed needle and thread to begin alterations while Alex was still in the tub.

Mister Young sat in the parlor reading a newspaper from Harrisburg. Iris joined him as she began her sewing.

"May I ask what happened to Alex?" she asked curiously.

"Nobody wanted her," he replied bluntly. "There was one couple who wanted her for a servant, but Alex begged me not to give her up to them. They looked mean and the man couldn't keep his eyes in his head. It gave me a bad feeling. But everywhere else, there was just no one interested. She's just too old and not as cute as the younger ones. She's quite upset, worried that no one will ever want her."

"That's so sad," Iris spoke her thoughts out loud.

"I offered her a job at the orphanage with wages. And I'd let her live in one of the staff rooms," he told his hostess.

"Did she accept?"

Mister Young nodded. "She didn't have a better alternative. She can tutor the younger children and help prepare the meals. I know it breaks her heart, she wanted a real family, but she could do worse. At least with me, she'll be safe and fed."

Iris looked down at the white printed dress. "I'm going to give her this. Maybe it will help cheer her a little." She smiled. "I best get her a robe to put on while I finish. Excuse me."

Iris went back upstairs for a dressing gown and undergarments. Outside the wash room, she tapped on the door. "Alex, it's me. May I come in?"

Alex lowered herself into the bath. "Yes, ma'am," she answered politely.

Iris opened the door. Alex was slumped down behind the wall of the tub to keep her modesty. "I've brought you a robe to put on once you're done. I'm working on altering a dress for you to wear, but it will take me a few hours. Here are some undergarments as well, for you to keep. This petticoat will make your dress flare out like you're wearing hoops. It will be very pretty, I think."

Alex stared in surprise. "Thank you, ma'am."

Iris nodded. "You are welcome. Come out when you're done, or stay in here if you like," she said with a kind smile.

"Thank you, ma'am," the girl spoke again. Then she added, "You've changed this room since we were here last."

"Yes," Iris smiled. "My parents are coming from South Carolina to live with me. My father lost a leg in the war and can't work anymore. They will be here next week and this is going to be their room."

Alex looked around. "It's nice. They will like it."

"I hope so."

Iris returned to her sewing. When the dress was complete, she returned to the downstairs bedroom. Alex rested across the top of the bed. The entire room smelled like honeysuckle. "Feel better?" Iris asked.

"Yes, ma'am. I think I must be dreaming. I've never been so clean or smelled so good. I almost feel ..." her voice trailed off.

Iris waited. "Feel what Alex?"

The young girl bit her lip. "Feel almost like a lady," she answered shyly.

Iris smiled. This poor girl. Iris knew what it felt like to have your life turn out differently than you planned or hoped for.

"Your new dress is ready," she offered, holding up the garment. "Why don't you try it on. Then I'll see what else I need to take in. Do you want help?"

Alex smiled at the fresh clean dress. "Yes, ma'am."

Already in the undergarments and petticoat, Iris helped the girl pull the dress over her head. Then she fastened all the hooks down the back. "You will need a corset soon," she told the girl.

Alex blushed, and said nothing.

"Hmmm. It's still too big on top and too long on the bottom. Why don't we eat first?" Iris suggested. "Then we can finish this afternoon. Do you want to come out in the dressing gown? It looks rather like a robe dress over your petticoat."

Alex nodded. "Mister Young is like a father to me. It won't matter if he sees me like this. As long as no one else is here."

"I'll keep Barney out of the house," Iris promised.

Hattie had prepared a good meal of sliced turkey, sweetened carrots, and herbed bread. Watermelon was for dessert. Alex ate heartily. Mister Young ate his share too.

"We haven't eaten this well in a long time," he confessed. "We only stay at inns when the price is good. Usually, we eat out over a campfire and sleep by the wagon. It's a real treat to be here."

"It sure is," Alex agreed quietly. "I wish I could stay here forever."

Iris was quiet as she thought about Alex's statement. Maybe she could stay. Iris would have to think about it for a while.

After lunch, the two females worked together upstairs to complete the dress. When it was ready, Alex pulled it over her head and twirled around in the room.

"Oh, it's so lovely!" she gushed. "Thank you, Missus Picket. Thank you so much!" She openly gave Iris a grateful embrace.

"You are welcome. What a different girl you are now from the one I saw this morning," Iris stated.

"Yes, ma'am. I feel like a new person."

"Let's do your hair now, shall we? Then we can go downstairs and work on that blueberry pie for tonight's supper."

Iris worked for ten minutes combing through the girl's blond hair. "What's your full name?" she suddenly asked.

"Alexandria Maria Parsons," Alex replied.

"That's a nice name."

"I'm named after both my grandmothers," the girl explained. "I never met them though. My parents moved away before I was born. All my grandparents died before I could meet them."

"I'm named after my mother's favorite flower," Iris confessed.

"What are your parents like?"

While pinning Alex's hair into a pretty chignon, Iris told her all about her childhood memories.

The rest of the afternoon passed with idyllic charm. After a wonderful supper, topped with blueberry pie, Iris and the house guests wandered into the parlor. Alex set herself beside Missus Picket.

"Do you like to read Alex?" Iris asked.

"Sometimes, ma'am."

"I have a Godey's Lady's book if you would like to look through it. I also have a mail order catalog from New York, if that interests you," she suggested.

"Yes, ma'am. I would like to look at them."

Iris spent several hours deep in thought that night. If she adopted Alex, she would have to give up one of the guest rooms. Also, since she was getting married, David should have some say in the matter. There was a chance he might not want a fourteen-year-old daughter. Maybe she could ask Mister Young if Alex could stay with her at least through the summer. That would give her and David time to decide if they wanted her permanently. Yes, she would ask.

After breakfast, Iris pulled Mister Young aside. "I would like to know if Alex could stay with me for the summer?" she asked.

"I don't know, Missus Picket. It might get her hopes up. Then when you send her back to me in the fall, she would be in a terrible state," he reasoned.

Iris put her hands on her hips. "Mister Young, I would very much like to adopt her, but I am getting married to Mister Stoneman and I want him to have a say in the matter."

"Oh? Congratulations. Where is he?"

"He arrives by train tonight with his family from Hartford. The wedding is to take place next week," she answered. "Also, my parents are coming to live with us from South Carolina. We are going to have a full house as it is, so I want to check with him first before I make such a big decision."

"What if I stayed on another night? Would that give you time to ask him?"

"Well, it would, yes, but I need your room tonight for his parents," she explained.

"Oh. I can move," he offered.

"But Mister Young, I need all the upstairs rooms tonight. His sisters are coming as well. The only room I have extra tonight is the one with the bathtub that I've prepared for my parents. I suppose you can have it, if you'll stay."

"Agreed," he nodded. "I shall move my things this very moment."

Nothing was said to Alex about their plans, except that she and Mister Young were to stay another night.

"Alex, I'm going to have a full house tonight. Would you mind sharing my room with me?" Iris asked the girl.

Alex's eyes lit up like she'd been offered the White House. "I don't mind, ma'am. Not at all!" Secretly, Alex was thrilled. She absolutely adored Missus Picket, and determined in her mind to pretend all night that the kind black-haired woman was her new mother.

"Let's go pick some wildflowers for the bedrooms. I have two baskets we can use."

All preparations were made throughout the day for the Stoneman family's arrival. Hattie worked in the kitchen making wonderful breads and other savory foods. Iris and Alex saw to it that the rooms were all in perfect order, and that fresh flowers were arranged in pretty glass containers.

Mister Young wondered at the transformation he saw in Alex. Overnight, she had become a pretty young lady, clean and neat. Her heart seemed happy too. He silently prayed that Mister Stoneman would agree to take her on.

That afternoon, Mister Young offered the use of his wagon. "Want me to drive?" he asked.

"Would you mind if Barney drove?" Iris countered. "If we all go, I don't know how we will get everyone and their luggage home."

The older man nodded understanding. "Alex and I will remain here."

Iris put on her pretty lilac gown. She wanted to make a good impression on his family. Her stomach was in knots though. She and Barney climbed onto the seat of the old wagon and headed toward town. She jumped half an hour later when the train whistle blew long and loud. It pulled into the station in a cloud of steam.

14

Iris and Barney waited for the Stonemans to come off the train. Iris began to worry when they did not unload with the other passengers in the main cars. She found one of the ticket men from the train. "Where are the Stoneman's?" she inquired.

He pointed to the back of the train, "In their car, ma'am."

Iris' eyes opened wide. They had their own car? My goodness! She had not realized they were so wealthy. What would they think of her rustic house? Of their son marrying a widow? A Southerner? Gracious! The knots in her stomach grew to the size of elephants.

Finally, David emerged from a carved doorway at the end of the car. He assisted his mother onto the platform, then helped his two sisters as well. His portly father came out, followed by two women who were obviously servants. The women in his family were dressed in fine silk and satin. Iris had on a silk dress, for which she was grateful, but it was very outdated from before the war. She had not invested in new clothing for herself lately because there were so many other expenses that needed to come first. After all, she was supporting herself.

David saw Iris and waved with a wonderful smile. Iris was glad to see him too, more than she could have imagined. David escorted his family to where she stood. He gave her a quick hug, then introduced everyone.

"Mother, Father, this is Iris Picket," he told them. "Iris, my father, Russell, my mother, Susan, and my two sisters, Constance and Rebecca."

"How do you do?" Iris greeted with a little curtsey. She noticed that his mother and sister Constance were looking down their nose at her.

"I've been better, frankly," his mother answered sharply.

"I'm so sorry. Was the journey hard?" Iris questioned.

"No quite," was her curt reply.

David then said, "This is Lillian and Beth, two of our maids."

Both women curtseyed politely. Iris gave them a friendly smile and said, "Welcome."

"Thank you, ma'am," they both answered at the same time.

"This is Mister Montgomery," Iris spoke, introducing her hired man.

"What a primitive town this is, Mother," Constance said so everyone could hear.

David shot his sister a nasty look, then glanced at Iris. "We brought quite a few things from home. It will take a while to unload. I also have quite a big surprise for you."

Iris stared at her fiancé with interest. He sure seemed different from his family. "Come, I will show you," he added, taking her hand.

Two men were opening the side door of a large box car. They led out two of the most beautiful black horses Iris had ever seen. Their hair was shining like satin. "How beautiful they are!" Iris observed.

"They are ours, dear," he confessed. "That is also," he said, pointing to another car where a beautiful carriage was being pulled down a ramp by four laboring men.

Iris' mouth dropped in surprise. "Oh!"

"Where's my trunk?" Iris overheard his mother demand.

"I'm sure they will bring them out in a moment," the elder Mister Stoneman replied.

"David, I can't believe this is yours," Iris whispered quietly.

"Ours," he corrected. "And I brought livestock to fill that barn too."

Iris looked at him in dismay. "I simply can't believe it!"

An hour later, three trunks, four satchels, one rooster and six laying hens were loaded inside Mister Young's wagon. Lillian and Beth sat at the back end watching the two cows and four pigs who were tied with rope to the wagon frame. The animals walked along easily, glad to be out of the train. Barney sat up front with the reins in hand.

Iris and the rest of the Stonemans led the way home in the fancy carriage. She was almost embarrassed as her friends gawked when they drove past. David waved to them from the front seat as he drove, unaffected by the carriage.

Sadly, Iris had chosen a seat in the back with David's family. She had hoped to get to know them, and form a friendship. However, it was a miserable ride.

"So, you're from the South?" Susan questioned.

"Yes, ma'am. Charleston."

"How unfortunate," Constance observed in a snooty tone.

Iris could not believe their rudeness.

"David told us your parents are coming to live ..." Rebecca began. She was cut off by a warning noise made by her mother. Susan scowled as she cleared her throat. Russell said nothing, but only looked around at the town and landscape.

Trying again to be polite, Iris spoke. "I fixed up all your rooms as nice as I could. I'm sure it won't be as grand as you're used to."

"I'm sure you are right," Susan snipped.

Iris gritted her teeth. Of all the ... She had a lot of nerve. At this point, Iris decided to remain silent. She looked out over the road and watched as the familiar trees passed by.

"Have you seen Sam lately," David finally asked from the front seat. He was furious at his family for being so rude. He had warned them to be kind, but he had met much resistance from all of them. Only Rebecca, the youngest sister, had a kind heart to match his own. She was only sixteen, and had not yet developed the uppity attitude society placed on its members. He would have a talk again with his parents and Constance before the night was over.

"No, I haven't. Not since the acting troupe came through," she answered.

"Oh. Was there a play?" he asked curiously.

"Yes. It was held outside, in town. We all had such a good time. They did Shakespeare," Iris explained.

"Shakespeare?" Susan gasped. "I'm impressed. I wonder though, did any of these mountain people understand it?"

Iris glared at her future mother-in-law. How horrid she was!

"Actually, yes, ma'am," came Iris' cordial reply. "You'd be surprised how many of us can read and write," she answered in a sweet as honey voice. Sarcasm, it was a gift.

David snickered only once from his seat. Iris had put his mother in her place. He was impressed.

"Humph!" Susan huffed. Then under her breath, she whispered to her husband, "Impertinent."

Iris was so glad to finally be home. David escorted her from the carriage first, then his mother and sisters. His father labored to get out on his own. Iris guessed him to be nearly two hundred and eighty pounds.

"Please, do come in," Iris continued her sweet southern voice. "I will show you all to your rooms."

David promised to bring in the trunks with Barney in just a few minutes. He was going to see to the animals first. So Iris was left to introduce the family to Mister Young, Miss Parsons, Hattie and the children. The Stonemans only nodded slightly. Rebecca smiled, but only when her parents weren't looking.

"Supper's ready," Hattie told them.

"Thanks, Hattie. We'll be back down soon. I just want to show everyone their rooms."

Mister Stoneman struggled up the stairwell, but finally arrived in the hall. Iris put David's parents in the master bedroom, it was the largest and most comfortable. She then showed his sisters their room.

"Where will David sleep?" Susan wanted to know.

Iris pointed to another door. "That is his room."

"Hump," came her disapproving reply. She shook her head and entered the bedroom, closing the door soundly. Constance did the same thing as her mother. Iris was left standing alone in the upper hall. They had only just arrived, but she was ready for this group to leave.

When Iris went back downstairs, she sought out Mister Young. "Sir, could I trouble you for a moment?" He gave her his full attention. "It seems the Stonemans brought two maids with them. I had not considered this and am now short of rooms again. Is there any way I can let you room here free tonight on my sofa in the parlor? I hate to put you out, but that back room holds two people and I have to make the best use of my beds," she explained apologetically.

David had entered and heard the last part of the conversation. "They can have my room," he offered gallantly. "Mister Young, keep your downstairs room. I'll sleep on the sofa instead, or in my carriage if I have to."

Iris looked at him sadly. "But, David ..."

"No. I should be downstairs anyway."

Mister Young spoke up. "If you don't mind sir, we can share. I can even sleep on the floor. I'm used to sleeping on the ground."

"No, you need the bed. I'll take the floor," David offered. There was no way he'd let that old man sleep on the floor.

"Well, thank you both. I'll put the maids upstairs," Iris determined. "That will work out better anyway. David, after supper, can we speak privately?"

"Of course. I'll get these trunks upstairs now." Barney came in and helped him carry the heavy loads.

An hour later, everyone sat around the table. Conversations went as well as could be expected. Iris felt completely snubbed by Russell, Susan and Constance. Rebecca was friendly enough, and tried to be pleasant. She and Alex sat beside each other, and seemed to get along well. After the meal, the two girls even excused themselves to go outside.

"Do you need my help, ma'am?" Alex had asked first.

"No, you go on," Iris answered. She wanted to encourage any friendship that was possible.

"Don't get your pretty dress dirty," Susan warned her youngest.

"Yes, ma'am."

Iris could see a lifetime of quiet compliance on the girl's face. It was easy to see she was the one bossed around by both mother and sister.

David ushered his parents and Constance into the parlor for a quick chat. He would insist they be kind to his fiancé. The two maids went upstairs to prepare the rooms for bed. Iris and Mister Young helped Hattie in the kitchen.

"You go visit with the folk," Hattie urged.

Iris shook her head. "Hattie, to be honest, I don't really want to. They're rude and snobbish. I don't know how David came from that family. I really don't."

"Lease they'll only be here a short while," the colored woman stated. "I heard that one girl say she was ready to leave already. And that she didn't want to stay one day past the wedding."

Iris shook her head with woe. "How are we going to put up with them for an entire week?"

Hattie grinned. "It's easy for me. I'll just stay busy. It's you I's sorry for."

"This too shall pass ladies, this too shall pass," Steve Young offered encouragingly. He then grabbed a dish towel and got to work.

After David's little talk, most of his family retired for the evening. Rebecca and Alex were still outside watching all the animals in the barn. They had a lantern to see, for it was now late and very dark.

David found Iris hiding in the kitchen. "Still want to talk?"

"Yes. Good timing too. We're done." She followed him outside for a slow walk down the road. They could see light coming from the barn and hear the giggles of both girls.

"I'm glad Rebecca found a friend," he spoke quietly. "She doesn't get to have much fun at home."

"I can imagine," Iris replied sarcastically.

"Listen, I'm sorry about the way they treated you this evening. They've no right. I had a talk with them after dinner. They should be better tomorrow."

"I hope so. I won't be able to stand it for a whole week otherwise. I won't tolerate them treating me so badly in my own home, even if they are your parents," she warned. "They haven't said one nice thing to me yet. Not even a thank you for supper, and Hattie worked hours on it."

"I know. I'm sorry," he offered simply.

Iris calmed herself with a deep breath. "David, that's not why I wanted to speak with you though. There's something else."

He stopped walking. "Is something wrong? Have you changed your mind about marrying me?" he worried, now that she had met his family.

"No. Not at all. I still love you," she assured him.

David reached for her hand. "Good. So what was it you wanted to say?"

"Well … it's about Mister Young, and Alex."

"Yes?" he encouraged quietly.

"Alex is the last one left. Nobody wanted her. You should have seen her yesterday when they arrived all dirty and tired. She was just forlorn, David. It broke my heart. I gave her a bath and a new dress and let her help me around the house. She's a new girl today and I was thinking, if you agree to it, that we could keep her. She's fourteen, and would be a great help to Mother and me."

"Do you want her?" David asked in a calm, quiet voice.

"I do, David. I really do. I want to give her happiness again, and all the things she's only hoped for all her life. But I'll only take her in if you want her too," she told him. "But if we don't take her, she goes back to work at the orphanage. I can't bear that thought."

David kissed Iris on the forehead as they paused in the middle of the road. "Well then, I think we should keep her," he spoke. "We certainly have the room. You can turn her into a lady too, I'm certain. And when the time comes, I'll find her a nice man to marry."

"Oh David, thank you!" Iris spoke lovingly. She wrapped her arms around his entire back and kissed him squarely on the mouth. David was taken by surprise, but was more than pleased by her response.

On the way back home, David asked, "Have you heard from your parents?"

"No, nothing more. I have their room all ready. It's the one you and Mister Young are sharing tonight."

"We're going to outgrow this house, I fear," he chuckled. "I think after the wedding, I'll build you another room for the bath tub. We can call it the wash house."

Iris giggled. "What about the bank? How are you going to find time to build it and a wash house?"

"I'm not building the bank. I've hired an architect for that," he explained. "They will arrive in ten days. Once it's up, we'll open."

Iris gave his hand a squeeze. "Sounds exciting."

"I contracted work with Sam to get the lumber. I assume it's almost ready now. That's why I was asking about him," David clarified.

"Guess he's been busy then," Iris stated. "That reminds me, remember the acting troupe I mentioned?"

"Yes."

"Margaret ran away with them when they left town. Her parents panicked and went after her, but she refused to come home. They get a letter every week. They say she's happy, but the whole thing was such a scandal."

This was surprising news. David raised an eyebrow.

"She got tired of waiting for a husband," Iris continued. "She didn't want to sit around here any longer so she set out to make a new life."

"I hope she's careful," David wished kindly.

Back at the house, David checked his watch. It was ten-thirty. His sister Rebecca and Alex were still giggling in the barn. Everyone else was asleep. He and Iris waited up in the parlor for the girls. Just after eleven, they finally returned.

"We didn't realize how late it was," Rebecca explained. She worried she was in real trouble.

David smiled. "It's quite all right. We're glad you two had fun out there."

"Guess we will go to bed now," Alex said quickly. "Goodnight."

"Wait," Iris stopped her. "Alex, we need a word with you first."

Alex's heart hammered in her chest. Was she in trouble? They didn't look mad. She glanced at Rebecca fearfully.

Rebecca waved and hurried upstairs. She hoped Alex wasn't in trouble. She liked her new friend very much. It was too bad she was going to have to return to the orphanage and work. At least they had promised to send letters to one another as often as they could.

"Don't worry, Alex," David assured the girl. "You're not in trouble."

They both watched as she breathed a sigh of relief. David allowed Iris to begin.

"Alex dear, I know how much you want to have a family of your own. And you know Mister Stoneman and I are getting married next week. We want to know if you would like to live here with us?"

Alex made a laughing noise in her throat. Then she ran forward and stopped in front of the couple. "Really? You want me? I definitely want to stay!"

Iris stood and embraced the teen. "Yes, we want you."

Happy tears fell from Alex's eyes and she could not stop smiling. This was exactly what she had wanted for so long. She never thought it would happen. But now, everything in her future looked better.

"You know what this means?" David asked the females. They looked up at him curiously. "It means we have to buy another horse so we can all go riding together."

Alex giggled. The Stonemans were going to be amazing parents. She could hardly wait!

Finally in bed, wearing a borrowed nightgown, Alex reached out and hugged her new mother. "Thank you," she whispered.

Sleepy, Iris patted the girl's arm. "You're so very welcome."

At dawn, Iris woke slowly. She dressed in blue calico and pinned her braided hair in spirals on top of her head. She fixed Alex's hair in the same way, making the girl feel quite beautiful. Alex wore the same cotton print dress from yesterday, it was her only one.

"We will go into town today and get you some more clothes," Iris informed her new daughter.

Alex smiled in delight.

Hattie fixed mouthwatering biscuits with jam and fried eggs for breakfast. David's family seemed a bit more sociable, but Iris could tell it was forced. She and David made the announcement about adopting Alexandria. Rebecca was delighted. The rest of the family was appalled, and tried unsuccessfully to hide their true feelings.

Susan Stoneman wondered how her son could possibly bring someone else's child into his family. He knew nothing of the girl's background. She was a dirt poor waif. What would it profit him to care for her? Honestly, what was he thinking? If Alex was to be a maid, then that would be tolerable. But a daughter? That was entirely different.

Once his coffee was gone, David told everyone he planned to go into town to find Sam. They had business to discuss. Russell decided to go as well. Iris then told David how she had promised to take Alex shopping for clothes. Rebecca volunteered to join them when she heard. And so the outing was planned, but first, Iris and David had papers to sign. Mister Young was leaving town as soon as that formality was completed.

Thankfully, Missus Stoneman and her awful daughter, Constance, decided to stay at the house. Both agreed there would be nothing at a country store that would interest them. Iris took Hattie aside and asked her not to leave mother and daughter alone in the house. She didn't trust them and figured they might go upstairs and riffle through her things, just for curiosity sake. Hattie brought all three of her children into the house to play in the kitchen while she worked. Susan and Constance quickly excused themselves into the parlor with their two maids.

David hitched up the team with Barney's help, but Barney offered to drive everyone into town. "It would be an honor to drive such a fine coach," he told them. For it was fine. The open coach was painted black with a fancy family crest painted in gold on the door. The inside seats were covered in heavy red velvet with woven tapestry lining the inside walls. On the narrow floor between the seats gleamed a thin layer of shiny polished black marble.

The three females took one bench, while David and his father took the other. Iris listened as Alex and Rebecca discussed school subjects. David and his father were deep in a conversation about money and investments. Iris smiled to herself and tightened the ribbon on her tall crown bonnet. It would be a fun morning. She had twenty-four dollars to spend on Alex and was sure they would use every penny.

The new buggy made quite a stir among the townsfolk. Patty and the doctor were there, finalizing plans for their own wedding in three weeks. They greeted Iris and David cheerfully and were introduced to his family, and Alex. Iris promised Patty an invitation to tea sometime before their wedding trip. Allen was taking his new bride to Philadelphia for two weeks.

Rose Reed walked up with a keen interest in the coach.

"Hello, Missus Reed," David called out. "Would you like a ride?"

"Oh yes!" she agreed with a broad smile.

He opened the door and helped her to a bench. Rose sat on the fine seat like a pleased young school girl.

"Iris, you lucky lady," the old woman said with a wink. "When I die, I want a carriage like this to take me into heaven. Do you hear that, Lord?" she asked toward the clouds. Then she giggled at her own joke.

Iris introduced the fun grandmother to everyone and told her about Alexandria's adoption.

"Well, you are a lucky girl, too!" Rose offered the girl.

"Yes, ma'am," Alex beamed in agreement.

Barney pulled up in front of the store and locked the brake. David helped each female from the back, then turned to Rose.

"Missus Reed, where is your grandson right now? I have some business to discuss with him."

"He just came home yesterday," she replied. "He's at the house."

"Very good. I'll be by this afternoon then," he decided. Rose nodded, and went into the store.

David turned to Iris and reached for her hand. He passed off the money discretely.

"Get what you need," he spoke quietly. He gave her a fun wink. "See you in a while."

Iris watched David walk away with his father. When she looked into her hand, she was surprised to see another forty dollars. Wow! That would certainly help. Quickly, Iris caught up to the girls. They were looking over some newly arrived bonnets.

"Rebecca, will you help us decide what Alexandria needs?" she asked. After today, she was sure the girls would be best friends.

"I'd be happy to help, ma'am," the sixteen-year-old answered. She reached for a blue bonnet and placed it on Alex's head. "Oh, so pretty."

The three females went through the store picking out two of everything. They chose a new pink bonnet and a nice straw hat trimmed with green ribbon. They picked out a good pair of tan outdoor shoes which buttoned up the front past the ankle, and a soft pair of light green slippers for wearing around the house. Iris also chose a new pair of stockings, a white apron and some ivory linen to make undergarments. She ordered a corset from a catalog and a hoop skirt so Alex could be properly dressed. Alex picked up a pair of soft kid leather gloves and several lengths of colorful ribbon to put in her hair. Finally, they came to the clothing. There were only a few pre-made dresses available at the store, and all were for grown women. They were simple cotton, nothing fancy. Iris went through them all. One had possibilities. She held it up to the girls.

"What do you think?" she asked, holding up the red plaid. "We could cut it at the waist and make a separate skirt. I think we should cut the sleeves short and cut the top down the middle and make a fitted bodice. We could trim it with ribbon and lace."

Not knowing, Alex looked at Rebecca. Rebecca nodded her head. "That would be good."

Alex smiled. "Let's get it."

Iris nodded and draped the dress over her arm. "Let's look through the catalogs for more. You'll need more than two dresses to make a wardrobe."

It was fun for all of them to pour over the drawings and descriptions in each catalog. Given the money she had, Iris was able to purchase everything, and order three more dresses. Five would be a good start for now. And once autumn arrived, they could order more made from heavier cloth. Iris knew she needed new clothes too, but that could wait for now.

She paid for the purchases as the girls gathered everything. Rebecca seemed just as excited as Alex over all the new pieces. In the coach, Alex changed into her new tan shoes. The old ones were falling apart.

"That was so much fun!" Rebecca admitted. "I wish you could come to Hartford. There are so many dressmaker shops, and the gowns are just lovely. Maybe one day you can come visit us."

"Maybe," Iris replied with a forced smile. She doubted it would ever happen. There was no way she would purposely want to spend time with David's parents.

As the females were waiting in the coach for David and his father to return, Tina Louis Shepherd walked by on her way to the telegraph and post office. She stopped to chat.

"My, what a lovely coach, Missus Picket," she complimented.

"Thank you, Tina. It was Mister Stoneman's back home in Hartford. He brought it all this way for us to use," Iris explained.

"And who are these lovely young women? His sisters?" Tina asked.

The girls giggled. Iris answered for them, "This is Rebecca Stoneman."

"Hello, ma'am," the girl spoke politely.

"Hello, dear," Tina returned.

"And this is my newly adopted daughter, Alexandria," Iris said proudly.

Tina's mouth dropped. "What a surprise!" she said happily. "Are you with the same group that came through last month?"

"Yes, ma'am," Alex replied.

"Well then, you will get to see the other four children at church on Sundays and at school this fall," Tina explained with excitement. "How old are you?"

"Fourteen."

"Good. We'll have you for at least two years of school then. I'm looking forward to it," she smiled.

"Thank you," Alex answered. "Are you the teacher?"

"No, I wish. I'm just the minister's wife. But I am on the school board and have four of my own children enrolled. I come to every event."

"Who is the teacher?" Alex wondered.

"Her name is Joanna Miller," Iris supplied. "She's the mother of my good friend, Bonnie. I think you'll like her very much."

Alex made a doubtful face. "Maybe. I don't like school much."

"It will be different here," Iris guessed. "Not like what you're used to at the orphanage. I imagine you will like it very much."

There was a little more small talk before the men returned, but regardless of what the women said, Alex was still not looking forward to school.

Six days passed. Alex was enjoying her new life at the boarding house. She helped with light housework, but nothing heavy. She was not a maid, Iris and David made that clear. All the while, they made plans for their wedding.

Iris' parents were due the following day. She had butterflies in her stomach just thinking about seeing them again. Somehow, through all her business, she had managed to avoid David's family quite a bit. Alex and Rebecca spent the days to themselves, talking girl stuff, they told everyone. Constance thought they were juvenile.

On this day though, Barney was taking the girls into town to meet the morning train. Alex's new clothes were due from the city. It made Iris wonder which train her parents would arrive on tomorrow because she did not know if they were coming in the morning or the evening. She would have to make two trips into town if they came on the second one. Once they arrived, Iris worried about how crowded her home would be. David would have to sleep on the sofa, or in the carriage. On the night of the wedding, Alex would have to take the sofa, or share with the Stoneman sisters. Somehow, she prayed it would all work out. For now, she needed to help Hattie prepare mountains of food.

That night, Alex tried on all her new clothes for everyone. Rebecca helped her with the corset and hoops. The first dress was a light blue silk, trimmed in ivory lace. It had short sleeves and beautiful pleats along the bottom of the skirt. A row of lace separated the sections of pleats and tucks. It was striking and very formal.

The second dress was made from a deep yellow linen, the color of apple cider. Small pearl buttons fastened the bodice down the back, with delicate beadwork on the front. Sleeves fit snugly down to her elbows and there were several layers of tucks around the hem of the skirt so it could be let out as Alex grew taller.

The final dress was a fine cotton print, more practical for everyday wear. The pattern was small flowers on a deep plum background. Attached around the neck was a small crocheted collar. It was very pretty with short sleeves and looked darling with the straw bonnet.

"I will teach you how to serve tea, now that you're a lady," Rebecca promised her new friend. The girls borrowed a tea service and went out to the porch to practice.

15

Iris paced back and forth on the wooden planks beneath her feet. She even chewed on the dry skin beside her fingernails, she was that nervous.

"You're making me anxious, Iris, watching you like that," David complained from his spot on a bench.

It was mid-morning, and they were waiting on the first train. Barney waited nearby in the black carriage.

"I just can't stand this waiting!" Iris whined. She continued to pace for another fifteen minutes while David counted her passes. She was up to fifty-four when the train whistled in the distance. Iris nearly jumped out of her skin. "Oh David, here it comes!"

She could hardly stand still there was so much adrenaline in her veins. She took hold of David's arm anxiously. She held his upper arm in a death grip as the train came to a stop at the station. Iris strained to look through the windows. She stood on her toes, looking around as passengers began to exit the doors. There were just a few people, however, and her parents were not among them.

Her heart fell. "Oh, David. They aren't here," she spoke in a wavering voice. So much hope had been in her heart to see them this morning.

"We can wait a few more minutes," David offered. "Your father may need help getting down. And if they aren't here, we will certainly come back tonight."

The trip home was a long one. David put an arm around Iris's shoulder for encouragement and support. She cried softly. "Tonight," he assured her. "They will come tonight."

The afternoon hours ticked by. Iris tried to find work to keep herself busy, but her attention span was very short. She kept looking at the clock, no matter how hard she tried not to. It was only three.

"Ugh! When is five o'clock going to be here?" she demanded out loud. Everyone in the parlor looked up in surprise. "Sorry," Iris offered. She put down her sewing and went into the kitchen with Hattie. "Give me something to do, please," she begged.

"Want to make lemonade?" Hattie suggested. She pointed to a large bowl of lemons. "Then you can serve it to everyone with these." She pointed to a tray of dainty cookies.

"Thank you, Hattie." Iris was so grateful. She got right to work.

Susan and Constance were appalled that the mistress of the house was serving tea like a servant. Nonetheless, they were happy to finally get some afternoon refreshments. Iris passed out glasses of sweet lemonade and placed cookies in napkins.

"Thank you, ma'am," Rebecca told her as she and Alex stopped looking over catalogs for a moment.

"Yes, thank you," Alex echoed.

"You're welcome girls," Iris smiled.

David thanked her as well, but no one else did. Iris thought about pouring the lemonade in his mother's lap. Wouldn't that be fun? She had to force herself not to giggle as she served the sour woman.

While they were all eating, Iris had an idea. "Alex, in a few weeks, how would you like to start a big sewing project with me?"

"What is it?" the girl wondered.

"Why don't we make a new quilt for your room?" she asked. "Would you like that? It will keep you extra warm this winter when the nights get cold."

"Yes, ma'am. That would be nice. I watched my first mother sew a quilt once. The cabin burnt down though before she could finish. I was only six then," Alex remembered.

Iris looked kindly at her new daughter. "Well this will be your very own special quilt. We can use scraps from your old dress and bonnet too, so it will have history."

Alex nodded approval of the idea.

Iris thought about quilting. "I haven't made one since I lived at home with my mother. What a long time ago that was," Iris said, quietly reminiscing. "She will help us."

"What's her name?" Rebecca asked.

"Savannah, after the town in Georgia," Iris replied with a smile.

"What is the South like? Will you tell us about it?" Rebecca inquired. "Mother says it's hot and nasty and full of ignorant white folk and mean darkies. Is that true?"

Susan let out a gasp at her daughter's impropriety.

David's eyes opened wide at the comment. Iris only laughed. "Certainly not, Rebecca! It does get hot down there, terribly hot, but the folks there are just the same as up here. You have your good ones and your bad ones," she answered, forcing herself not to look directly at Susan. "There are some who are rich, just like up here, and some who are poor. Some go to school, some don't. It's the same as everywhere else."

"What about slaves? Did you own any?" Rebecca continued curiously.

"Rebecca, you keep quiet!" Russell demanded.

The girl's face flinched.

"Actually, I don't mind answering," Iris said calmly. "Yes. My husband and I did own slaves, but only a few. My husband was a crop broker and we lived in town. We didn't have a plantation where many workers are needed to bring in the crops. Some people we knew owned over a hundred slaves. Hattie was my house slave. I brought her with me when I ran away and gave her freedom when she got married. I now pay her to help me run things here."

"Was Mister Montgomery yours too?" Alex asked.

"No. He came along a year later," Iris answered.

The girls continued to ask questions about the South. Iris gladly answered each one and in no time at all, it was five o'clock. David stood and said, "It's time to go again."

Iris was surprised at how fast the questions had passed the time. "I will tell you girls more about the South another time. Thank you for keeping me busy."

Iris checked with Hattie before leaving. Supper would be ready upon their return. It was a special meal of roasted duck, buttered potatoes, green beans, sliced tomatoes, and fresh rolls.

Barney drove into town again. This time, however, Iris sat on the bench with David. Her leg bounced nervously and made the wood squeak. Dark clouds gathered in the distance. David hoped they would all make it home before the rain arrived. Otherwise, they would have a mess in the carriage. He made a mental note to purchase a closed carriage before winter arrived.

The train whistled. Iris stood up and looked down the track. She smiled with anticipation. Half an hour later though, she was crying into David's shoulder in the back seat of the coach. Her parents had not arrived again. She was now both disappointed, and worried. What had happened? Where were they? Iris cried all the way home and went directly upstairs to her room without a word to anyone. She left David to explain.

Hattie and the two maids served supper to the rest of the family. David said the blessing, asking God to watch over Iris' parents and keep them safe. He also asked for word of their whereabouts. The meal was eaten with more silence than usual. Eventually, David took a tray up to Iris' room.

He knocked quietly, not wanting to wake her if she was asleep. Iris opened the door and let him in. "Hattie wanted me to bring you some food," he offered sympathetically.

"I'm not very hungry, David," she warned with a gentle voice.

"Still, it's here if you want it." David set the tray on a side table and walked over to the bed. He sat down on the edge and patted Iris on the shoulder. Quickly, she crawled up into his arms and wept against his chest.

"Shhh," he soothed. "They probably just got delayed for some reason. Anything can happen when you're traveling. Maybe they decided to stop somewhere and rest an extra day. You just never know," he offered, trying to calm her fears.

After a few minutes, Iris regained control of her emotions. She gave him a weak smile. David kissed her on the forehead before letting go. Iris walked over to her dresser and pulled out a handkerchief. She blew her nose as quietly as possible. "Thank you for bringing the food. Will you give everyone my regards downstairs? I think I want to be alone tonight. I'm not feeling very sociable."

"Certainly. May I check on you before bed though?" he asked. "I won't come late, I know you will probably fall asleep early."

She nodded. "Thank you, David. It's nice to be cared for."

David kissed her once more before leaving the room. Iris undressed and put on a thin nightgown followed by her comfortable dressing gown. She opened her window all the way to let in the cool night air. It was not yet dark, only seven, but the evening breeze was blowing gently. Iris pulled a chair in front of the window and sat down. She could smell rain from a nearby storm. Slowly, she removed the pins from her hair. Grabbing her brush, she began to pull it through with long strokes. Finally, she plaited it in one wide braid and secured it with a wide ribbon. After fifteen minutes of staring out the window, she decided to eat. Iris was just finishing the meal when she heard horse hooves coming up the road. She listened carefully as they came closer. Her window faced north, away from town, so she could not see anything. But below, someone knocked on the door.

Iris ran to her bedroom door and cracked it just enough to listen.

"Telegram, Mister Stoneman," she heard a familiar voice say. "For Missus Picket."

"Thank you," David replied.

Iris was already on her way down the stairs in bare feet. "A telegram? For me?" she called out.

David gave it up quickly. Iris unfolded the paper and read the words.

"Tomorrow!" she shouted happily to everyone. "They will be here tomorrow. They were delayed in Philadelphia. Oh, I'm so glad they are safe. David, you were right."

At ten the next morning, David and Iris stood on the platform as the train pulled into the station. Heavy clouds hung low in the sky and threatened more rain. David worried again about the ride home.

Only a handful of passengers came down the steps. Iris pointed. "There they are!"

David saw a thin woman with graying hair supporting a man who was hopping down the steps with one leg. A railroad employee stood behind them with a wheelchair. Iris rushed over with David two steps behind.

"Mother! Father!" she shouted without thought of propriety.

They looked up and smiled broadly. "Iris!" her mother screamed. She ran over for a tight hug. The two females embrace in tears for over a minute. Iris then released her mother to give Tom a tight hug as well. He was crying, too.

"It's so good to see you both," Iris spoke through laughing tears.

"You look so good honey," her mother said with pride. "Just beautiful, as always."

"I can't believe you're here. Finally here! I was so worried yesterday when you didn't come," Iris confessed.

Thunder rolled in the distance. David cleared his throat.

"Mother, Father, this is Mister David Stoneman," Iris introduced quickly. David shook Tom's hand and Savannah's as well.

"Are you the Mister Stoneman who was so kind to help us?" Savannah questioned.

"Yes, ma'am."

Tom put his hand on David's arm. "I can't tell you how grateful we are."

"I was happy to do it," David replied.

"Mom, Tom," Iris spoke slowly. "David is just a wonderful person. And he's asked me to be his wife."

Savannah's hands shot up to her mouth. "Really? Oh my goodness! How wonderful!" The females embraced again.

Tom congratulated them and asked, "When's the wedding?"

David grinned and glanced at his future in-laws. "Tomorrow, actually. We were waiting for you to arrive."

"I'm so glad you waited," Savannah sighed.

Another long low thunder rolled across the sky. "I guess we had better get your things and get going before the sky opens on us," David suggested.

"All we have is one bag, I'm afraid," Tom confessed. He pointed to a satchel on the platform.

Iris grimaced. Her parents had had so much in Charleston – a home full of things and plenty of clothes to wear. Tom used to have a good business too. To be reduced to one satchel was heartbreaking.

David looked at Tom. "Sir, should I push your chair or carry the bag?"

Tom was not too thrilled about a Yankee soldier pushing him, but he knew Savannah could use the break. She had been pushing him around for months. He would swallow his pride again. "The bag isn't too heavy. We can put it on my lap, then you can push us both."

Iris carried the bag. David pushed Tom to the end of the platform and down the ramp.

"How far do you live?" Savannah asked her daughter.

"Not too far mother, about three fourths of a mile. But we have a carriage."

"You've done well for yourself, Iris," Tom complimented. "That's commendable."

"Thank you, sir."

David pushed the chair to the carriage. Barney hopped down and opened the door. Iris introduced him to her parents. "He married Hattie, my maid. Remember her?"

"Yes," Savannah smiled. "How is she?"

"She's well."

Tom lifted himself inside the carriage with his arms and one good leg. He was impressed with the ride. "Nice carriage."

"Thank you sir," David stated. "I plan to get a closed one before winter."

"How cold does it get here?" Savannah asked with a little worry.

"Quite cold, Mother. Several times it stayed below freezing with three feet of snow on the ground," Iris answered.

"Goodness! We never saw anything like that in Charleston."

Iris and David sat together on the seat opposite her parents. David secured the chair in front of him. Barney tapped the reins and drove home quickly as more thunder rolled overhead. It was just beginning to sprinkle when Barney pulled into the yard. David helped everyone down and brought the satchel inside. Barney saw to putting up the horses and carriage while Iris introduced everyone in the parlor. She could tell that David's parents were watching hers with contempt. She wanted to smack them for it. Iris knew what they were thinking – poor white trash from down South. Dirty, stinking rebels. Iris' only consolation was the knowledge that his parents were leaving the day after tomorrow. And not a minute too soon.

Tom wheeled himself over to Russell and offered a handshake. He hated to do it, but he had to swallow his pride. He was indebted to the Stonemans for opening up the account. It was a great service done, considering their political differences and geographic loyalties. Tom spoke a few kind words to David's father. Russell just accepted his thanks without much conversation.

"You have such a nice home, Iris dear," Savannah observed. It was arranged nicely with comfortable furnishings, pretty rugs, and good drapes.

"Thank you, Mother. It needed a lot of work when I first bought it, but we find it comfortable now," Iris replied humbly. She continued introducing David's sisters, who smiled politely. Then she brought Alex up front. "Mother, Father, I want to introduce my newly adopted daughter, Alexandria."

Tom raised an eyebrow. Savannah smiled kindly. "Glad to meet you, dear."

Alex curtseyed. "Thank you, ma'am."

Savannah made a noise in her throat. "I suppose that makes me a grandmother, in a way. Gracious!" The family shared smiles and a little laughter. The three snobbish Stonemans looked terribly bored.

"Would you like to see your room now?" Iris asked. "You can rest or refresh a while before we eat at one. Hattie is preparing something special for you."

The parents agreed and were led to the room off the kitchen. Good smells filled the air. Once her parents were situated in their room, Iris went upstairs to find some dresses to lend her mother. She had discovered that her mother had only two left, and both were terribly worn. She wondered what exactly had happened to reduce her parents to such a state. They had had such a comfortable living before the war. Iris was sure she would find out eventually. For now, she was just grateful to have them in her home.

Iris pulled out the cream and peach dress, and a blue striped cotton one. At the last minute, she reached for another and yanked the summer print from the cabinet as well. Her mother would have to do with three for now until more could be ordered. It was obvious that Tom needed new clothing too. Maybe they could get into town tomorrow before the wedding.

After the mid-day meal, Iris and her parents spent the entire afternoon catching up on all they had missed in the last four years. David shared in the conversation as well, wanting to know more about his new family. Alex and Rebecca had escaped through the rain to play in the barn. The Stonemans and their two maids went upstairs to be alone. Iris was delighted.

She learned from Tom how the cannon shrapnel had ripped open his leg during the attacks on Charleston in sixty-three. After infection set in, it was removed in a most horrid way. It had taken him months to recover. And once he did, he could not find work of any kind. Slowly, they ran out of money and accumulated debt. Savannah had even taken up washing for the soldiers and other people in town to earn a small wage. But when the entire town was evacuated this past February, they had lost their home and nearly all its contents. They relocated to a small house outside of the city and simply survived day by day. In May, they had finally given up their last servant. They were at their lowest when Iris' letter had arrived. It gave them their only hope. The money that soon followed had been an answer to prayer. Of course, Tom wasn't happy about having to move north and live among the enemy that had destroyed him. But he knew for the sake of his wife and their survival, that he must go.

Iris told her parents about her adventure north with Hattie, and about life in Williamsport. She also told them how she came to be Alex's new mother.

"How noble of you to take her in," Savannah commented.

"Yes. Very kind and generous," Tom agreed. "Just as you are to take us in."

Iris gave him a smile. "I wouldn't have it any other way."

David smiled, pleased and proud of his future bride. She was a good person, through and through.

Conversations continued through a light supper and late into the evening. Around nine, David asked Iris to sit with him on the porch for a while. Everyone else retired for the evening.

The night was pleasantly cool after the day's rain. Iris took her chair and breathed in the freshness. "It always smells so good after it rains," she shared contentedly.

"Yes, it does," he agreed. "I wish we could walk, but your dress would get ruined."

"We can walk another night."

David was quiet for a moment before speaking. "Can I ask you a question?"

Iris looked at him in the darkness. He sounded so serious. "Of course you can."

He cleared his throat. "I've noticed that you've given away four of your dresses in the last week or so. How many do you have left?"

He was very observant for a man. "A few. Enough," she replied. "I might need a few new ones for fall."

"How many do you have?" he repeated.

Iris took a breath while she mentally calculated. "Only one for winter, the lilac ball gown, my mother's old mourning dress, my new wedding dress, and three others."

"So you have three?" David questioned.

"For now. Once I order more for mother, I will take mine back."

David frowned. "Iris, when was the last time you bought yourself some new clothing?"

"Before the war. I can't remember exactly," she confessed. "I've had other more important things to do with my money."

David rocked in his chair. "I just want you to know Iris, that tomorrow, when you become my wife, that your finances are secure. You won't have to worry about money any more, and I'm going to see to it that you and your parents get new clothes, for every season."

How wonderful was his generosity! "Thank you, David. You are very kind."

There was a comfortable silence between them while they listened to the crickets in the grass.

"Are you nervous about tomorrow?" David finally asked.

Iris shook her head. "No. Not at all." It was the truth.

David smiled. "Good. Me either. I'm honored that you'll have me. And Iris, I promise never to hurt you. I'll always be a man you can be proud of."

Iris reached over, placing her hand on his. "I am proud of you, David. And I love you more than you know."

"I love you, too."

16

August 4, 1865

"I can't wait to get out of this village, Father!" Constance called out as the family rode to the church. "I hate it here. There's nothing to do!"

"I know, dear," her mother soothed. "Only one more day to bear and we will go home. No more sickening Southerners! I just don't see how your brother could love one of those people."

"I'm quite fond of her mother," Rebecca spoke quietly. "She's nice."

"Rubbish!" Russell Stoneman stated. "Who needs nice? She's from a Southern family with no funds. What does she bring to this union? There's no dowry, no wealth. Just a small house in a tiny village. What good will that do us? Our friends back home will never receive her."

Rebecca was not surprised by what she was hearing. Her parents and sister were terribly conceited, self-centered people. "Father, you know as well as I do that Iris' home is one of the largest in town. She's quite well respected here," she defended.

"Child, that is of no consequence. Her home isn't as big as our servant quarters!" Susan spoke harshly. "It will just be a great relief to me when this is over and we can leave."

Barney listened to this conversation with growing anger. How could they be so heartless. He was proud of Rebecca for trying to stand up to them. He wondered whether or not to share this conversation with David. They had become friends and respected each other greatly. Being a hired man however, he kept his mouth shut for the present moment and quickly drove his passengers to the church. Besides, he was anxious to return home for Hattie and the children. They were going to the wedding too.

David, Alex and Iris' family were already in town. They had gone in earlier that morning to go over catalogs at the store. David had slipped away at one point to send a telegram to Philadelphia. He would not tell Iris what it was about, but told the family to all buy two new sets of clothing. Alex understood that she already had five summer dresses, and that was sufficient for now. David had promised her more clothes before winter.

Tom and Savannah could not believe David's generosity. They almost hated to take more charity from him, but he insisted. Tom chose for himself two fine suits, a new hat and a pair of gloves. David also privately told the clerk to order men's underclothes and a nightshirt as well. Savannah and Iris both chose one cotton dress from the store, and ordered a second from a catalog. Again, David secretly ordered underthings.

After shopping, the entire party proceeded to the church. David and Iris brought their wedding clothes and planned to change at Doctor White's house. Tom, Savannah and Alex were going on to the church to decorate with Iris' friends. Alex wore the light blue silk and felt very rich indeed. Tom wore his only clothes because he was much too frail to fit into David's. Savannah wore the pretty peach and cream dress. It was the nicest she had worn in months.

At four o'clock, the church was filled with guests. It seemed the entire town had come out for this much anticipated wedding. There would be a feast on the grounds afterward. Alex and Bonnie stood at the front as bridesmaids. David had Sam by his side. The preacher was ready and waiting as the bride entered. All eyes turned as Iris came into the room in her beautiful new ivory gown. David smiled wide with pride. She was beautiful and wonderful.

Wildflowers and blue banners adorned the room, but Iris only had eyes for David as she watched him through the lace veil. Happy tears slid down her cheeks as she walked forward.

The service was completed in twenty minutes. David raised the veil with anticipation, and kissed his lovely bride. Nearly everyone clapped with pleasure. Iris smiled with happiness. The congregation stood as the newlyweds walked down the aisle. Within minutes, the churchyard was full of friends and family.

Iris made a point to avoid eye contact with David's parents. She wanted this to be a good day with nothing to spoil her fine mood. All but the Stonemans came with hugs and kisses for her good fortune. While the receiving line grew, several of the women began to set up the food table. After a meal, there was to be dancing.

Iris was surprised to see so many people with gifts. She had not expected many, maybe just a few from her closest friends.

Just around seven-thirty, when the dancing was under full swing, Sam climbed the church steps and banged a metal spoon against a pail. It made an awful racket, but gained everyone's attention.

"Attention! Attention!" he called loudly. The crowd hushed. "As the best man, I am obliged to say a few words. What we have here tonight is a celebration of two of my closest friends. I know you will join me in wishing them both much happiness and many years together. You know, I could be jealous over David's good fortune, because Missus Stoneman is such a beautiful woman. But if I can't have her, then David is the next best choice," Sam paused as his audience chuckled and murmured. "He is the next best choice because he is good and honorable and I owe him much." Sam lifted his drink in salute. "So let us say thank you to these two good people for giving this town so much of themselves and send them on their way!"

"Hurray!" several men shouted. Applause and smiles swept through the crowd. Iris shook her head at Sam, then smiled at her new husband. She was caught unaware as someone lifted her off her feet. Iris looked up to see the young Doctor McCory.

"What are you doing?" she demanded. "Put me down!"

Allen McCory only smiled and carried her to an awaiting wagon. He put her down in the back without ceremony. It was then that she noticed two men carrying David and forcing him into the wagon as well. As soon as David's back hit the boards, the wagon took off. Iris yelled out for someone to help as she reached for the sides. She stared at David with real fear. To her surprise, he was grinning.

"What's happening?" Iris demanded. Her heart pounded in her chest.

"Sir, where are you taking us?" David asked the driver in a loud voice.

"Special delivery!" the man shouted back as he sped down the road which led out of town.

Iris frowned as she recognized the shop keeper's voice. What on earth was going on?

"Where are you taking us?" David asked, knowing now that some joke was taking place.

"It's a surprise," the store owner chuckled. "Just wait and see."

After five minutes of mad running, the driver finally slowed the tired horses. Iris looked around, not recognizing her surroundings. "Where are we?" she asked.

"You'll see. Almost there," he explained.

"Who arranged this?" David wondered.

"The whole town. We all had a part," the man explained. He turned the wagon up the mountainside on a winding road. Iris and David both held on to keep from slipping out the back. Finally, the wagon leveled off and turned one final corner.

Iris' mouth dropped as an open valley came into view. She could see for miles. In the small clearing where the wagon stopped, there was a small one room cabin. It was very rustic, but neat and tidy. She smiled with pleasure.

"Your wedding cottage!" their driver told them with a tip of his hat. "Why don't you get out and look around."

David slid off and reached for Iris. He pulled her gently to the ground after such a harsh and bumpy ride. As soon as her feet hit dirt, the driver tapped the reins and pulled the wagon around.

"See you later," he called jovially. Iris and David watched in disbelief as he sped away.

Once he was out of sight, they looked at one other in astonishment. "What a view!" Iris exclaimed. The sun was floating over the horizon in a sling of orange and yellow.

"I agree," David answered, staring into her face.

She smiled as blush filled her cheeks. David came closer and reached out to touch her face. Beneath their private sunset, David kissed his bride once more. After several moments, he scooped her into his arms and carried her into the cabin.

At noon two days later, Barney arrived to take the newlyweds home. He grinned in amusement as they climbed into the carriage.

"Thanks for the ride, Barney," David spoke. "Did you know about this cabin?"

"Yes, sir, I did. In fact, I helped deliver some of the food here a few days back," he answered proudly.

"Who owns this little house?" Iris wondered.

"Missus Reed, ma'am. It belonged to her brother-in-law. This was her gift to you, but your friends helped her get it ready."

"We will have to do something nice for them in return," Iris spoke softly.

David nodded and turned to their driver. "Did my parents leave yesterday?"

"Yes sir. Woke me up at dawn demandin' to be taken to the station. I was sure in a fix trying to get ready fast as they needed it."

David scowled. "Sorry about that, Barney. I figured they would hurry home."

"Poor Alex and Rebecca though," Iris sighed. "They got along so well."

"Yes. She's a lot like me, Rebecca," David declared. "Nice on the inside." He gave his wife a playful wink.

"Maybe they can get together for holidays," Iris thought out loud.

"At least," David agreed. "And they can write every week." He settled back into the seat and put an arm around Iris' shoulders. "What about Tom and Savannah? Are they getting along with Alex?"

"They are all just fine," Barney assured the couple. "They were talking about a quilt this morning. And the ladies were working on a dress that Miss Rebecca left for Alex."

"A dress?" David asked.

"Yes sir. Seems Miss Alex admired the pink dress Miss Rebecca wore on your wedding day. So yesterday morning, before your family left town, Rebecca gave the dress away. It was all a secret though until after the train left town."

David chuckled. "My mother won't like that. It will ruffle her feathers for sure. Poor Rebecca. I'll do what I can to get her here again before the end of the year," he promised his wife.

And Barney drove them home.

Over the next week, the large, new family settled into a new routine. Alexandria had her own room upstairs, with a fine bed, an oval rug, and lace curtains. The cabinet against one wall contained her dresses, shoes and other clothing. Her hats and apron hung on hooks. She spent the last of her summer days writing letters to Rebecca, playing outside, or sewing. Already, she had begun to cut up pieces of her old dress and bonnet for her new quilt.

David and Iris moved their things into the master bedroom. That left only two to rent out. David asked his new bride if she wanted to continue the boarding house, and she told him, "Yes." After all, the town needed a place for visitors to stay. That gave David an idea. Maybe he could build a hotel near the train station. That was doable. He would make inquiries the next time he went into town.

As far as their marriage was concerned, both newlyweds were happy together. Iris no longer feared the days or nights. With David, she was blissfully contented. And David wasn't complaining. He absolutely loved being married to the woman of his dreams.

Tom and Savannah acclimated to their new surroundings with relative ease. They made several new friends in church on Sunday, and seemed genuinely happy to have a good life again. David had even taken Tom horseback riding through the countryside. The injured man was able to ride well, despite his missing leg. And to cinch their new in-law relationship, David offered Tom a job at the bank, when it opened. He would easily be able to sit behind a counter, manage paperwork, count money, make loans, and get to and from work on a horse. Tom accepted, pleased to have his ability to earn an income restored. Iris ordered her father a fancy crutch, which would make getting around even easier.

On the morning that the architect and work crew were due to arrive, David asked everyone to join him in town. All but Hattie and her children accepted the invitation. She preferred to remain at home for a little extra playtime.

"Where is the bank going to go?" Alex asked on the way.

When David described the lot, Iris smiled. "That's where the play was last month. Good spot."

Barney pulled up to the station as the train whistled in the distance. David smiled in anticipation. It was a big day for surprises.

The entire family watched as the black machine came to a stop. A side door opened on one of the cars. Sixteen men jumped down while one shouted orders. All of them hurried to a back car and began to unload. David recognized his architect.

"Aren't you going over?" Iris asked.

"Not yet," he replied. "I'm watching out for some other passengers too."

"Who?" Iris questioned curiously.

David grinned. "It's a secret."

Iris looked puzzled, but turned to see who stepped off the train. By her side, David lifted his arm and waved. "There they are," he spoke. "I think."

He walked toward a group of three women holding satchels. Two mustached men stood behind them. They all looked foreign, with olive colored skin.

"You are the Lombardi Sewing Company?" David confirmed.

"Yes sir," one female replied, "at your service. Mister Stoneman?"

"Yes. That is me. Have you any other luggage?"

"Oh, yes, sir. Six crates," one of the men supplied.

Iris looked up at her husband. Alex simply stood in awe.

David turned to explain. "I decided that the family needs a proper wardrobe. So they are here to sew for everyone, including the Montgomerys and your parents.

Alex squealed and clapped her hands. Savannah and Tom Payton stared at this Yankee with wonder. Was there no end to his generosity?

"Oh, David!" Iris whispered. "You are so good."

David spotted the preacher who was standing nearby with his wagon. "Would you be willing to help us carry everything home? Our carriage is only big enough for the ladies."

"Be glad to help," the kind man replied. "What's in these crates?" he asked a few minutes later. "They weigh a ton."

"Sewing stuff, I guess," David answered. "Machines, fabric, lace ..." Once everything was loaded, David turned to his wife. "The Lombardi's will be staying with us for a few weeks while they work. Do you mind returning with them to the house while your father and I stay here? We have much to do with the architect."

Iris nodded and kissed him on the cheek. "See you tonight."

When Tom and David arrived at home about supper time, they each carried a parcel. "The new clothes arrived that we ordered on our wedding day," David announced.

Savannah opened the package to pass things out. "We didn't order these undergarments," she spoke shyly.

"I ordered them. There's enough for everyone," David explained.

Alex grabbed a mint green nightgown that was just her size. "Oh, how lovely!" She ran over to her new father and gave him a hug. "You're the best."

He smiled with satisfaction. "How did it go today with the Lombardi's?" he questioned the family.

"They are resting right now," Iris explained. "But they showed us the pattern books and we opened several of the crates. They are in the dining room. It's all a mess with satin, linen, velvet, cotton, wool and so much more. We just don't know where to begin."

"They are all so beautiful, too," Alex added. "Such colors and patterns! I don't know how I'll be able to choose from all the ribbons and lace and buttons and trim." She actually sounded delighted to have such troubles. It was only days ago she was down to her last filthy dress. How quickly her life had changed.

"I've ordered enough for everyone to have at least eight new outfits made," David explained to everyone in the room. "Plus coats and capes for winter. I don't want it said that I don't take care of my Southern family." He gave Iris a wink. He would always care for her, always.

Hattie stood in the doorway smiling.

"That includes you too, Hattie," David clarified. "You, Barney and all the children are getting new clothes."

Hattie's mouth dropped open and she nearly dropped the dish of peas in her hand. Dinner was quickly forgotten. She ran to tell her husband and bring her children inside.

Two hours later, the meal resumed. The family had to eat in the parlor due to the sewing supplies all over the dining table. The Lombardi's requested to eat outside on the porch. They wanted to breathe in some fresh country air.

"Where do we start with it all?" Alex asked her new grandmother.

"Just take your time," Savannah urged. "You will probably change your mind several times before finally deciding. But we will help you. Iris and I have done this before."

Iris watched as her mother offered advice to Alex. She then looked at her stepfather, who was eating his second plate of food. She had seen a change in him just these last few days. His health was improving by leaps. Maybe it was the mountain air. Maybe it was the love in their home. At last, Iris turned to her husband, her beloved husband. She could not imagine loving him more than she did already. How wonderful it was, this second time around.

EPILOGUE

Christmas 1865

Alexandria sat in the parlor working on the last stitches of the quilt she planned to give Rebecca for Christmas. It, as well as the new one on her own bed, was made from scraps of all the new clothing which now hung in closets all over the house. Both quilts were beautiful creations, and Alex was anxious for her friend to arrive in a few days. She would be staying with them for two entire weeks.

As for the Lombardi's, it had taken them two months to complete everything. Part of the delay was due to the fact that by the end of September, Iris realized she was with child. Her dresses had to be redone entirely to accommodate an expanding waistline. She and David, along with the rest of the family, were delighted over the prospect of their first child. Iris had wept that first night, thankful at last to be a mother.

David's bank was prospering. He and Tom worked diligently, offering loans to customers, helping them save money and make wise investments. David made wise investments with his capital as well. Not only had the bank doubled its money with Sam's lumber business, but also increased their holdings with the addition of a new restaurant and hotel near the station. Hired help managed the businesses efficiently.

As predicted, Alex enjoyed school. She made good marks and several new friends. Learning had become fun and easy now that her home life was so happy. She had a family to please and praise her work too. Iris and David were very proud. It made all the difference in the world.

Once Rebecca arrived, the family would attend the church social. Iris knew a secret that would transpire just before the anticipated event. Sam had confided in her that he planned to ask for Bonnie's hand in marriage. They had spent much time together at her wedding in August, and had continued growing their friendship through the fall. Sam had even been able to convince Bonnie to stop wearing the low cut dresses. With his business doing so well, he had the money to fix up his grandmother's home, adding two more large rooms before the first snow fell. Rose was delighted at gaining a granddaughter-in-law, if there was such a thing. She adored Bonnie as much as Sam did. As for Rose, she still corresponded with Doctor White's father.

Constance Stoneman had turned nineteen and accepted a proposal from a wealthy merchant in Boston. She was married in November at a grand ceremony with all of high society in the pews. David and Iris sent their regards and a nice mantle clock.

Life was good in Williamsport. Iris had overcome her past and created a new life which was happy and satisfying. David had a lot to do with it.

June 1869
Alexandria's Wedding

On Alex's eighteenth birthday, twenty-one-year old Edward Benjamin Brighton proposed, and was jubilantly accepted. The Brighton's owned the Harrisburg newspaper and were comfortably wealthy. Edward was the fourth in line of seven sons. He and Alex had met two years earlier when she attended the Culbertson Academy for Ladies during a special summer session on music and art. Iris thought it a good idea for Alex to be instructed in such things as a lady should know. Because of the baby, Iris had no time to teach her. After meeting at the opera house, Alex and Eddie were practically inseparable. Over the next two years, their friendship grew. Alexandria went to Harrisburg with her family when she could, and Eddie made reasons to visit Williamsport as often as he dared. Through letters and arranged meetings, their love grew. The couple was to live in a three-story, brick home in Harrisburg, but they would be just a few hours away by train. Either family could visit often.

Currently, the modest church was full of guests from both towns. Iris and David quite liked Eddie's family. They were very agreeable people.

David held his squirming three-year-old daughter, Tabitha, in his arms as they waited to enter the church. Tabitha was to be the flower girl, while David was, of course, giving the bride away. Iris helped a nervous Alex with her veil. Little seven-month-old James David was nearby, cradled in the arms of his nanny. He was the newest member in the Stoneman house and gave both his parents fits. David had hired the nanny to help Iris take care of their fussy son. James David was poorly tempered, even at this young age.

Iris knew that when the ceremony was over, all their guests would ride in buggies to the Stoneman's new home. It had just been completed this past spring on a new lane in town nick-named "millionaires row." All the men who had gained fortunes in the lumber business lived there, including Sam Reed. He and Bonnie, with their two children, lived just two doors down. Iris was proud of her new six-bedroom home with its formal dining room and grand parlor. She looked forward to entertaining this Christmas season. Besides her parents, who were still living with them, the family shared the house with four servants: a new cook, a maid, the nanny, and a butler. David and Iris had given Hattie and Barney the old house. Hattie had fainted when she found out and none of them let her live it down. Hattie now stayed home and raised her three children. Barney worked for Sam as a foreman at the lumber mill.

Iris thought about the friends who would be in church today. Margaret had returned to live with her parents after divorcing her actor husband. They had one child together who was now two-and-a-half. He was a very naughty boy. Margaret was much humbled by what she had gone through, finding her husband cheating on her several times before finally leaving him. She kept mostly to herself now, too ashamed to even socialize with her once closest friends.

Patty and Allen were still happy together. They had one surviving child, a little girl. Claire was two and sweet as sugar. Patty had lost two other children, a boy to fever and a stillborn girl. But still, they hoped for more. The loss had been hard on them both, but Allen most especially. As a doctor, it broke his heart not to be able to save his own children. However, their faith was strong and they had hope.

David's younger sister, Rebecca, would be in the church as well. She and Paul, her husband of one year, were expecting their first child this fall. Alex was delighted that they had traveled all the way from Washington D.C. where Paul worked in government. Alexandria and Rebecca had remained close friends these four years, writing often and visiting whenever possible. Alex had even been a bridesmaid in Rebecca's wedding, regardless of Susan Stoneman's disapproval.

Iris thought about her own wedding nearly four years ago and how good life had been since. She hoped and prayed that Alex and Eddie would know the same kind of joys. She was happy to know life had turned out well for her adopted daughter. She would continue to be happy and well cared for. How lucky she was to have come from such poor beginnings, to be so richly loved. How lucky they all were indeed. Iris looked heavenward, thanking God for everything.

ALSO BY THE SAME AUTHOR

What's in
YOUR
purse?

Prayer is the key
to our
intimate
relationship
to God

Coming for Valentine's Day 2013:

Please Love Me

MORE FROM ENERGION PUBLICATIONS

Fiction

Covenant	Daniel Martin	$17.99
Megabelt	Nick May	$12.99
Prayer Trilogy	Kimberly Gordon	$9.99
Stories of the Way	Henry Neufeld	$9.99
The Traveler's Advance	Heath Taws	$14.99

Personal Study

Holy Smoke! Unholy Fire	Bob McKibben	$14.99
The Jesus Paradigm	David Alan Black	$17.99
The Sacred Journey	Chris Surber	$12.99
When People Speak for God	Henry Neufeld	$17.99

Christian Living

Faith in the Public Square	Robert D. Cornwall	$16.99
Grief: Finding the Candle of Light	Jody Neufeld	$8.99
I Want to Pray	Perry M. Dalton	$7.99
Soup Kitchen for the Soul	Renee Crosby	$12.99
Crossing the Street	Robert LaRochelle	$16.99

Bible Study

Learning and Living Scripture	Lentz/Neufeld	$12.99
From Inspiration to Understanding	Edward W. H. Vick	$24.99
Luke: A Participatory Study Guide	Geoffrey Lentz	$8.99
Philippians: A Participatory Study Guide	Bruce Epperly	$9.99
Ephesians: A Participatory Study Guide	Robert D. Cornwall	$9.99

Theology

The Politics of Witness	Allan R. Bevere	$9.99
Ultimate Allegiance	Robert D. Cornwall	$9.99
History and Christian Faith	Edward W. H. Vick	$9.99
The Church Under the Cross	William Powell Tuck	$11.99
Journey to the Undiscovered Country	William Powell tuck	$9.99

Generous Quantity Discounts Available

Dealer Inquiries Welcome

Energion Publications — P.O. Box 841

Gonzalez, FL_ 32560

Website: http://energionpubs.com

Phone: (850) 525-3916